BAG OF BONES

Helen Cresswell was born in Nottinghamshire, the middle child of three. She started writing poems and stories at the age of six and has not stopped since. She has had a varied and successful career since leaving university, during which time she has been a literary assistant, a teacher, and worked prolifically for BBC television. She is the popular author of *many* stories for children and adults and has been in print for thirty-five years.

Helen has two grown-up daughters and a grand-daughter, an use in Nottinghamsh

Also available from Hodder Children's Books

Owl Light
Maggie Pearson

Spilling the Magic
Stephen Moore

Similon
Kathryn Cave

Goblins in the Castle
Bruce Coville

BAG OF
BONES

HELEN CRESSWELL

*Hodder
Children's
Books*

a division of Hodder Headline plc

A Catalogue record for this book is available from the British Library

ISBN 0340 67302 8

Typeset by Hewer Text Composition Services, Edinburgh
Printed and bound in Great Britain by
Mackays of Chatham PLC, Chatham, Kent

Hodder Children's Books
A Division of Hodder Headline plc
338 Euston Road
London NW1 3BH

For Jack and Marion with love

ONE

Griselda Dogberry was nine years, three months and two days old when it happened. Her brother Tom was eleven and six months and three days, and her sister Alice had been seven for only a week.

You needn't think that Griselda was pleased with her name, because she wasn't. She would have liked to have been called Samantha or Charlotte or Victoria. At least then you wouldn't get called Grizzles or Grizzly.

As soon as Griselda was old enough she had asked her mother why she had picked that name.

'It's unusual,' she had replied. 'And it sounds like someone out of a fairytale.'

But Griselda Dogberry was not someone out of a fairytale. She and her brother and sister and mother lived at number 27 Lime Street in a perfectly ordinary row of houses with a view of the gas-works at the front and a park at the back. There wasn't a palace or a woodcutter's hut or a gingerbread house in sight.

Griselda wasn't against fairytales; in fact quite the opposite. She often sat reading them while Tom sat yelling and zapping in front of his computer.

That is exactly what they were doing on the first day of their half-term, when this story begins. They didn't *know* it was going to be the beginning of a story, of course. I don't expect people ever do.

Griselda read four stories, then wanted to go to the park, but Tom wouldn't. He had just been given a new computer game.

'People go blind staring at those things,' she told him.

'And reading books. They go blind reading books.'

'They never!'

'They do!'

'Don't!'

'Do!'

They could keep this up for hours. Downstairs, Alice was watching a cartoon. She did this a lot.

'You'll get square eyes doing that,' Griselda
told her.

'Won't!'

'Will!'

'Won't!'

'Will!'

'Anyway there's nothing else to do,' said Alice.
'And shush – it's just getting to the good bit.'

In the end Griselda went to the park on
her own.

'Don't go further than the swings,' Mrs Dogberry
told her.

She said this every time. It was so she could keep
an eye from the kitchen window.

'Shan't be long,' Griselda said. 'It's not exactly
exciting. It never is. I wish something really exciting
would happen.'

She had better look out. You'd think people
who read a lot of fairytales would know better
than to go wishing things.

'If wishes were wings, we'd all be kings,'
said Mrs Dogberry vaguely. She too had read
a lot of fairytales when young, and was rather a
romantic.

'Queens in your case,' Griselda corrected her, 'and princesses in mine.'

'Oh clever clogs!' said her mother.

'I suppose in your case you could say if wishes were beans we'd all be queens, but I can't think what you'd say in mine. What rhymes with princesses?'

'Oh go on with you! And just look out in that park. People get murdered in parks, remember.'

'I can think of quite a few people I'd like to murder,' said Griselda. 'But I wouldn't necessarily do it in the park. Bye – back for dinner!'

As she wandered along Lime Street towards the park she had a go at finding a rhyme for 'princesses' but soon gave up. Instead, she made a list of people she'd like to murder, starting with Sharon Parker. She soon had a very satisfactory list. It went like this:

1 *Sharon Parker* Horrible ginger hair pulled out by roots. Force-fed with worm sandwiches, then dropped in boiling oil.
2 *Kevin Tate* Forced to write 'I am a know-all and dirty dobber' one million eight thousand and ninety-two times. Then eaten alive by giant ants.

3 *Paul Roberts* Forced to buy hundreds of packets of crisps to give back to people he's pinched them from. Then locked up and starved to death. (This would probably take yonks. He wasn't exactly a hairpin to start with; more like a dustbin on legs.)

4 *Miss Murdoch* (Griselda's teacher at Witherspoon Road Junior) Tied up and made to wear earphones belting out the Top Ten non-stop. If this doesn't kill her, death by dinosaur.

Having just seen the Murdoch off, it was quite a shock to hear her voice from the grave.

'Good morning, Griselda.'

There she was, pointy nose, specs and all.

'Oh! Morning Miss Murdoch!'

'And are we enjoying our half-term?'

'I don't know,' replied Griselda truthfully. She certainly was, but couldn't speak for the Murdoch.

'It's nice to see you out and about in the fresh air,' Miss Murdoch said. 'Too many children will spend the week hunched over their computers, I fear.'

'Tom is,' said Griselda meanly. Not that it mattered. He had left the Murdoch's class two years ago. Now he had Mr Chubb, who wore an Everton scarf and picked his nose when he thought no one was looking.

'Try to find something useful to do, Griselda,' Miss Murdoch told her. 'Something sensible.'

'OK,' said Griselda airily, and Miss Murdoch walked on.

Griselda Dogberry had not the least intention of doing anything sensible. What she was looking for was something the exact opposite, something . . . something *wild*. She didn't know what, but thought she might know when she found it. The park seemed as good a place as any to look.

But when she reached it, it looked boringly ordinary and the same as usual. There were boys from her school kicking a ball about because when they grew up they all wanted to play for Man United. There were kids swarming all over the playground area, swinging and sliding and whizzing round. They seemed to be having a good time, but that was not Griselda's idea of having a good time. She wanted something really exciting to happen for a change. She sort of kind of wanted the world to go topsy-turvy. She wanted ET to land smack in the middle of the football pitch, or a pack of wolves to come loping out of the bushes.

Fat chance, thought Griselda glumly. She was stuck here in the boring old real world, which looked more boring than ever after the fairytales she had just read. No wizards or dwarves or wolves or witches – just a bunch of kids who wouldn't even know how to begin slaying a dragon if they saw one.

Oh I wish, don't I just wish, there was a dragon! she thought. *Or something!*

There she goes again, wishing. Admittedly she didn't do it out loud, but a wish is a wish . . .

She had no sooner made it than everything changed. The park didn't turn into a wild wood or the kids suddenly sprout wings. It was nothing as obvious as that. It was as if she had been looking at the world through a blurry window, and now everything swam into focus. She suddenly noticed the peeling paint on the metal railings, and when she looked at the grass every single tiny blade seemed to stand up stiff and separate.

'Oh wow!' said Griselda Dogberry. 'What's happening?'

Because something definitely was. The sun's rays

13

came striking down like spears through the trees, and it was brighter and yellower than it had ever been. The whole park was floodlit gold and all the yells and screams had turned to ghostly echoes. She looked down at her own hand and saw each freckle amazingly brown and perfect, as if it were important. She saw a blackbird pecking and felt as if she could count its feathers, and when the worm came up it was so deliciously pink and gleaming that she could almost have eaten it herself.

Griselda felt as if she were on tiptoe at the very edge of something, and was holding her breath. She felt like you feel when the blue touch-paper of a firework has been lit, and you're waiting for it to go off, to start fizzing red sparks or go whooshing up into the sky. If you make a wish, it is very like lighting the blue touch-paper. (Not, of course, that Griselda knew that. At her house, only her mother was allowed to light it.)

So there Griselda stood, in this sudden crystal world, and she didn't know what was happening or what she was expected to do. So she did exactly what most people in her shoes would have done – she started putting one foot in front of another.

She had no idea where she was going, or why. She wasn't sleepwalking, though. She saw that the path beneath her feet was winking and throwing off sparks, and tarmac had never done that before. Before she reached the bandstand she stepped from the path and into the shrubbery, and some of the leaves that brushed her were old and dusty and some were new and shiny, and they were all marvellously criss-crossed and complicated. It was as if the whole world was filled with millions and millions of leaves and now they were jumping to meet her because she had never noticed them properly before.

She didn't think; she was all eyes and amazement. If she had been thinking, she would not have gone into the shrubbery at all. Griselda knew full well that murderers lurk in bushes, and kidnappers. Her mother had told her so a hundred times. And if Mrs Dogberry had been looking out of the window to keep an eye on her daughter, and had seen her step into the bushes, this story would never have happened at all. Any story begins with a particular person being in a particular place at a particular time. And if Mrs Dogberry had seen what was happening, she would have gone running down and called over the fence, 'Griselda, you come out of there, you hear me? Come out of those bushes this very minute!'

And then Griselda would never have found it. She very nearly didn't find it anyway. She was too dizzy, too amazed by how suddenly the world had sprung to life. She was too busy noticing how the bark of trees was like a lunar landscape, and the sunlight was crammed with a billion swarming motes of dust and thick enough to stir. She stretched up her hand and watched them dance at her fingertips.

Then she noticed the watch on her wrist, and that also seemed larger than life and amazingly shiny. It was an old one, though, an old-fashioned one she had borrowed from her mother only a week ago, when her own broke.

'Silly old thing,' Griselda had said at the time. 'Stupid hands – it's even got a stupid second hand!'

'It tells the time, that's the main thing,' Mrs Dogberry had told her. 'And you've got no idea of time at all. At least you'll be here on time for your meals. And don't break it, you hear? I like it, even if you don't!'

Now Griselda gazed at the watch and noticed the

rubbed edges of the strap and the tiny scratches on the dial, and then she noticed her own wrist and saw that the skin was not smooth, as she had supposed, but daintily pitted and with tiny blue veins running into her hand.

'Hello, wrist,' she said. 'Hello, hand!'

She didn't usually talk to herself like that. She was in a very strange state indeed, and part of her knew that. But another part felt absolutely at home, as if all at once she had come where she belonged.

She gazed at the dial of the watch and it was striking fire in the sunlight. She gazed and gazed until anyone might have thought that the dream turn of the second hand had sent her into a trance.

But the second hand was not moving. It had frozen at an exact point between the five and the six. And if the second hand was not moving, it almost certainly meant that the minute or hour hands weren't either.

Griselda did not think, Oh help, now I'm for it! She didn't even give her wrist a shake, in case the tiny finger had got stuck. She simply thought it very likely that time was standing still, and she wasn't even surprised. If time was holding its breath, it probably felt exactly the same as she did. The whole world was waiting for something to happen.

When Griselda noticed the bag she did not realise at first that this was the something. There it lay, under the broad leaves of a laurel. It was made of cloth of a faded bluey grey, and was tied at the top with a grubby drawstring. It looked as if it could have been there for centuries. She sat down at the side of it and waited to work up courage to do what she most certainly was going to do, which was — open it.

It occurred to her that this was the biggest surprise she had ever had in her whole life. It was going to be even better than opening a birthday or Christmas present. This dusty old bag could contain absolutely anything, there didn't even seem much point in guessing what. But she did. She guessed treasure, gold coins and winking jewels. She guessed at such riches that Mum would never have to go to work again, and they could move to a house with a huge garden and a room each for everyone. (Griselda had to share a room with Alice, but would rather not.) Griselda put out a finger and gingerly touched it and felt the rough grain of the fabric. Then she prodded it. Whatever was in there seemed to slither, and there was an odd, dry rattle.

Griselda's eyes fixed on the knotted cord and she felt her heart come right up to the back of her throat.

Here goes! she thought. *Let the cat out of the bag!*

She started to pick at the tight knot. She picked and piggled till at last the cord was loose, then pulled one end and it lay curled on the ground.

She did not put a hand inside the bag. It was not crocodile-sized; it was not even *baby* crocodile-sized. Whatever was in there could not possibly be alive. All the same, she wasn't going to put her hand in it. As a matter of fact she rather wished Tom was there, or even Alice. She suddenly felt lonely, on her own with that bundle.

If I sit here much longer thinking about it, she thought, *I'll probably never open it at all.*

Which would be a pity. She had wished for something exciting to happen, and now it had. She did not like to think of herself as a rabbit. So she made herself a dare. She dared herself to open the bag. First she got up on to her knees, to make it easier to run if she needed to. She leaned over the bag and took one side of the opening in each hand. She drew a deep breath and slowly, ever so slowly, drew her hands apart.

'Oh!'

She gasped and dropped the cloth again. She had caught only a glimpse but that was enough. What she had seen in that fleeting instant was – bones! A jumble of white bones, of all different shapes and sizes. They might have been human but they might have been those of a cat, dog, sheep – anything!

But who had placed them in a hessian bag and pulled the string tight? And was whoever that person was . . . a murderer?

'Oh help!' said Griselda. She didn't know what to do. On the whole, she thought, she had better go home.

Then she heard it.

'Help! Help!'

The voice was faint and plaintive and it wasn't coming from anywhere out there in the park. It was coming from the bag of bones.

'Let me out! Let me out!'

Griselda jumped to her feet.

'I'm out of here!' she said, and ran.

Two

A person who has just found a bag of bones under a laurel in the park, and then heard it speak, is in a very strange state of mind. Griselda was nearly back home before she even realised she was. She had simply been putting one foot before the other as she had when she'd walked into the shrubbery in the first place.

She stopped suddenly and looked down at her watch. The second hand crawled steadily round the dial. She looked about her, and saw at a glance that the world had gone ordinary again. The tarmac under her feet was dull and grey, the grass limp and the sunlight pale. Griselda felt a pang. She had liked that brand-new world glimpsed a moment ago – was it only a moment ago? She wanted to go back there.

She walked on slowly, thinking about the bag of bones. Why was it there? Why, when she found it, had the whole world changed and her watch stopped? Why, if it was hundreds of years old, had the gardeners not found it long before now? And why – and this was the biggest why of all – had it spoken to her?

She realised that, although she was running away from the bag of bones already, she wanted to be back there with it.

Not on my own, though, she thought. *I'm not being a coward, just sensible. If all three of us go, it'll be safer.*

It was not easy to explain what had happened.

'A bag of *what*?' asked Tom.

'Bones,' repeated Griselda, and Alice shrieked.

'Was it dead, was it someone murdered?'

'I don't know,' Griselda told her. 'But listen, that's not all.' They looked at her. This was going to be the hardest part. 'It . . . it spoke.'

There was a little silence. The ice-cream van was ringing its chimes in the street below.

'You're off your trolley,' Tom said, at last.

'I'm not! It did, really it did!'

'What . . . what did it say?' Alice quavered.

'Well, first it said, "Help!" and then, then it said, "Let me out!"'

'Thought you said there were only old bones in there!' Tom said.

'There were! There were! I don't get it either! But then it spoke and . . . and I ran for it!'

'So would I,' said Alice with feeling.

'You don't *believe* her?' said Tom. 'You know what she's like.'

'Why should I make it up? I wouldn't even have *dreamed* of finding it. I just did. And anyway, you can see for yourself.'

'Not me, thanks,' Tom said.

'I wouldn't mind,' said Alice, 'not if all three of us were there. Did it really speak, Grizzles?'

'Really,' Griselda told her. 'And the only reason Tom won't come is because he's scared.'

She knew it would work, and it did.

'Right!' he said. 'Come on!'

So the three of them went to the park and Mrs Dogberry decided to go shopping, because three children are safer than one, and in any case she didn't believe much harm could come to them in the park.

'It wasn't an ordinary bag,' Griselda told the others as they went. 'Not a plastic supermarket

23

one, I mean. It was made of cloth, a proper drawstring bag.'

'There wasn't any blood on it, was there?' inquired Tom, and Alice shrieked again.

'No there was not,' Griselda told him.

'Were they big bones or little ones?' asked Alice nervously.

Tom knew what she was thinking. 'Well they can't have been a dinosaur's,' he said. 'Use your loaf. That's if there *were* any bones. Now . . . where were they?'

Griselda looked about her. One part of a shrubbery looks very like another. Only a short while ago it had seemed as if every single leaf was different. Now they had all gone identical again. She walked a few paces, looking for clues, though she knew there were none. She took her bearings from the bandstand.

'Here, I think,' she decided.

'Come on, then,' Tom said. 'Let's get it over.'

The three of them pushed in among the bushes. Alice at least was on tiptoe and ready to run.

'It was under a laurel,' Griselda said. 'Look for a laurel.'

'What d'you mean, look?' Tom said. 'There are billions of them. There's—

He stopped dead. Griselda peered past him.

'Oh, thank goodness!' She had been half afraid that it would have gone. Once it was out of sight, she had almost stopped believing in it herself.

They stood and stared at it, all three. It was not like any other bag they had ever seen.

'Ten out of ten, Grizzles,' Tom said. 'So far.'

'Can we go, now we've seen it?' Alice asked. 'I don't think I want to see any bones.'

'Well I do,' Tom said.

He dropped to his knees beside the bag. Then he parted the top exactly as Griselda had done earlier, and just as swiftly dropped it.

'There you are!' Griselda was triumphant.

'I don't get it,' Tom said. 'Why would anyone put a load of old bones in a bag and dump it here?'

'I don't ... I don't think they're *ordinary* bones,' Griselda told him. She couldn't explain, and didn't want to, about the way the world had changed in the twinkling of an eye. And she was certainly not going to tell about the watch stopping.

'What we could do is take 'em home and piece 'em together,' said Tom. 'Like a jigsaw.'

'Can't be human. Not big enough.'

'I don't think Mum would like it,' Alice said. 'That bag's dirty. And she won't like us playing with old bones.'

'No need for her to know,' Tom said. 'We just take it home and shove it under the bed or somewhere. Then, after dinner, we'll have a go at it.'

'But what if it comes alive! It *spoke*, she said!'

'That's true,' admitted Tom. '*Did* it speak, Grizzles?'

'Yes it did. I didn't invent the bag, so why should I invent it speaking?'

'It might . . . it might be listening to us now,' said Alice in a whisper.

Griselda herself thought it very likely. She thought the bag had a deep mysteriousness. It contained more than any of them could possibly guess. She would not in a million years have dared pick it up herself and take it home. But now she knew that that was what they must do.

'Go on, then,' she told Tom.

She knew that it must be picked up, but did not much feel like doing the picking. She, after all, had heard the voice. Even Tom hesitated.

'It's not as if it's pinching or anything,' he said. 'Someone's just dumped it.'

'And bones aren't exactly valuable,' Griselda added.

'Well they're not going under *my* bed!' Alice said. 'Pull the string tight, Tom, so whatever it is can't get out!'

Tom took either end of the cord and pulled it tight. Then he lifted the bag and they heard the bones slither and chink. They all felt gooseflesh rise on their arms and necks.

'Come on!' Tom said. 'Let's do it!'

They pushed their way out of the bushes and were out in the open again. Everyone else was kicking a ball or walking a dog or swinging. They alone had a a secret, a deep dark secret.

'Dem bones dem bones dem dry bones!' Tom sang, and swung the bag.

'Don't!' Griselda told him. 'Don't shake it!'

'You might hurt it!' Alice trotted behind, trying to keep up.

'Hurt what?' Tom was scornful. 'You can't hurt a load of old bones!'

'Don't say that!' Alice pleaded. 'It might be listening, whatever it is!'

'And pigs might fly!' he told her.

And so they might – or so it seemed to Griselda, who alone had heard that plaintive, mewing voice.

It was easy enough to smuggle the bag into the house. Mrs Dogberry was grilling sausages for dinner, and did not even glance at the three of them.

'Had a nice time?' she asked, in the kind of way that meant she already took the answer for granted, and would not even have heard if one of them had replied, 'Yes, actually. We found this bag of old bones, and now we're going to try to piece them together.'

They all trooped up the stairs, Tom leading. He went into his room and put the bundle on the chest of drawers, and again they heard that curious dry chink. They stared at it. Even at home, in the everyday world, the cloth bag did not look ordinary. It seemed unnaturally still and surrounded by its own mysteriousness.

'Under the bed,' Griselda said. 'Better.'

So Tom took the bundle and pushed it out of sight. Mrs Dogberry's voice called, 'Dinner!' and they all went down.

They were halfway through the rice pudding with apricot jam when their mother said, 'Well . . . first day of half-term, and I've got a surprise!'

They all looked at her.

'Ice rink!' she said. 'Then McDonald's, and then to a movie! What do you think?'

It is sad when a person arranges a treat for people who are not in a mood to be treated. The young Dogberrys had their minds fixed on a bag of old bones.

'Er . . . great,' said Tom at last.

'Ace, Mum,' said Griselda weakly.

'Does it have to be today?' wailed Alice.

'Well! That's nice, I must say. Didn't you hear? Ice rink, McDonald's, movie!'

It did sound good. And the bones, after all, were not going anywhere. The young Dogberrys decided to accept their fate with a good grace. They went along to the ice rink, they nobly champed their way through burgers and ice-cream sundaes, then trooped off to the cinema to watch the movie they'd all been begging to see for weeks now.

By the time they got home they had almost completely forgotten about the bag of bones. The whole thing seemed far away and unreal. In any case, it was bedtime.

'We'll have a go at them in the morning,' Tom told the others.

'You're not going to sleep with them under your *bed*?' Alice was shocked.

'Course, dumbhead. Why not?'

'Rather you than me,' said Griselda, and meant it.

'Girls!' said Tom, as he often did, and 'Boys!' said Griselda automatically.

So they went to bed, and soon their mother put out the lights and went to bed too. One by one the lights in all the houses in Lime Street went out. The roofs and pavements gleamed under the curious muddy mixture of moonlight and sodium streetlamps.

It was round about midnight when the bones

under Tom's bed began to stir. They made hardly any sound, yet all at once, Tom, who had been fast asleep and dreaming, found himself sitting bolt upright in bed, eyes open, wide awake.

He heard the soft chink and slitherings, and knew at once what it was. 'Help!'

He sprang off the bed and in a flash he had reached the door, was over the landing and in the girls' room.

'What's up? What's up?' Griselda was fuddled with sleep.

'Wake up. And Alice. Wake up!'

'What? What is it?'

'Ssshh,' Tom hissed. 'You'll wake Mum!'

'But what—?'

'The bones.' He clapped his hand over Alice's mouth just in time. 'They're moving!'

'What d-d'you mean?' Griselda knew very well what he meant. In a way, she was not surprised.

'I can hear 'em rattling! Come on!'

Griselda scrambled out of bed and seized Alice's hand.

'Just stay near me,' she whispered. 'You'll be all right.'

'But I don't like skelingtons!'

'We're here in our own house and we can always yell and wake Mum. Come *on*, Alice!'

'She's a baby,' Tom said.

He knew it would work, and it did. All three of them went tiptoeing back to Tom's room. Once inside, he carefully closed the door. In the dimness they could see the bed, and they looked fearfully over to it.

'Can't we have the light on?' pleaded Alice.

'No. Too risky. Mum might see. Hang on.'

Tom crossed the room, giving the bed a wide berth, and pulled back the curtains.

'That's better!'

It was, but not much. The light was pale and foggy, and it gave everything a queer bleached look. Their own faces were waxy and unfamiliar as masks.

Then they heard it – the chink and slithering of those dry bones. Then came the voice.

'Help! Help!'

Alice clutched fiercely at Griselda.

'Let me out! Let me out!'

They could not simply ignore it. They were

32

well-mannered children and to do so would be plain rude. On the other hand, it is rather peculiar to hold a conversation with a bag.

'Who are you?' asked Tom at last, and his voice came out as a croak.

'Let me out! Let me out!'

'The needle's got stuck,' Tom said. 'Can't it say anything else?'

'Pull the bag out and leave it open, and perhaps it'll get out by itself,' Griselda suggested.

So that is what Tom did. He took the very tip of the bag by the very tips of his fingers, and gently tugged it out from under his bed. Then he dropped back rapidly and waited. This time, when the bones moved, they all actually saw the cloth moving. It heaved and rose and sagged.

'Let me out! Let me out!'

'It's never going to stop!' said Griselda desperately. 'We'll have to let it out!'

'So what do we do?' demanded Tom. 'Just tip it up over the carpet? Shut up, Alice!'

Alice was squeaking again.

'I suppose,' said Griselda dubiously. 'What else?'

At times like this she was glad she wasn't the

eldest. It went without saying that Tom was the one who would have to do the deed. It was at times like this that he wished he were not the eldest.

He moved slowly towards the heaving bundle. His sisters were pressed close against the door; Alice was feeling for the handle. All at once Tom stooped, grabbed the bag and tipped it upside down and stepped swiftly back.

The whitish bones tumbled and flew, and clicked softly one against another. They lay quite still on the carpet in a haphazard jumble. For what seemed like ages there was absolute silence.

'Now what?' whispered Alice at last.

'We've let it out,' said Griselda. 'That's what it asked us to do, and we've done it.'

'*I* have, you mean,' Tom said. 'But look at it – dead as a dodo!'

'I can hear you!' came a voice.

All three jumped. Griselda swallowed. 'We can hear you, too,' she said. 'But all we can see is some old bones.'

'Ah, but that's not really me,' came the voice. 'Would you like to see what I'm really like?'

'Er, yes. I suppose so,' said Tom, though he was not quite sure that this was true.

'Then you'd better say so!' came the voice. 'All three of you. Go on, say it!'

They exchanged anguished looks. They were in a corner. Not one of them now would dare scoop up the bones and put them back into the bag. Something must happen, or they would all still be standing there by morning.

'Er, I'd like to see you,' said Tom boldly.

'And me – please,' said Griselda. She nudged Alice.

'And me!' she squeaked. 'But please don't be anything too terrible, and please don't . . .'

Her voice trailed off.

The bones were glowing, giving off a white searing light like a lunatic moon. And they were moving in a slow deliberate dance, gliding, rearing up, joining one to another. The longest bone rose and lay curved and floating in thin air. All the rest of the bones came smoothly round it, and slotted into place like a jigsaw making itself. At last there was a skeleton, and it was of an animal. By now the whole room was filled with dazzling light.

Then in a kind of melting blur came flesh and fur, curling whiskers and plumy tail, and the soft round pads of paws.

'It's a cat!' breathed Alice. 'It's a great big golden pussy-cat!'

She stepped away from her brother and sister and went towards it as if she were sleepwalking, with hands outstretched. And as soon as her fingers went into the dense, gingery fur, there came the rumble of a deep and growling purr, a purr that seemed loud enough to wake the street. Because the cat was no ordinary cat. It was huge – half the size of Alice herself, and more like a lion cub than a cat, except for the fur, because it was most wonderfully furry.

'Oh, puss!' Alice was ecstatic. 'Oh beautiful pussy!'

She dropped to her knees and put her arms round its neck and could actually feel the purr. It stood quite still and its mouth seemed to curve into a smile. Over Alice's head Griselda met its eyes: they were not green, but gold.

'I don't believe this!' Tom said.

'Then you had better,' said the cat.

Alice, startled, dropped her arms and squatted there staring up at it. The purr faded and rumbled into silence.

'You talked! Cats don't talk!'

'Wrong!' said the cat, and drew itself up stiffly.

'Oh don't be cross! I just mean *ordinary* cats don't!'

'Nobody could call you ordinary,' Tom said.

'You . . . You aren't by any chance the Cheshire Cat?' asked Griselda.

'Certainly not,' replied the cat haughtily.

It started to prowl about the room. It trod deliberately, its plumy tail waving. It sniffed disdainfully and dabbed with its great round paws. The trio watched and waited. At last it had finished its explorations and turned to face them.

'So this is the world, is it?' it remarked.

They were foxed by this curious question.

'Well, part of it, I s'pose,' Tom said.

'Then I don't think much of it!' the cat said. 'You had better open the window!'

They exchanged anguished glances.

'You can't jump out!' Alice cried. 'It's too high!'

'Open the window!' it repeated, and its manner was so lordly that it seemed impossible to obey. Tom went slowly over.

'Oh, don't go!' begged Griselda, but the window was already open, and the cat sprang up to the sill with a graceful leap. 'Shall we see you again?'

'That', replied the cat, 'is up to you!'

It crouched for an instant, then leaped, and as it went the light in the room went with it. Alice let out a wail, and then that wail froze, and all of them froze.

Because the cat had not jumped down to the pavement. It had launched itself into air and was flying – or rather treading on air, because it had not suddenly sprouted wings. They crowded at the window and watched it as it went, over the roofs and chimneys and past the silvery spire of the church, as if following an invisible path in the night sky. It was as if light had been pitchforked among the stars, it flashed and flickered about the stalking cat. On and on it went, till it was only a speck beyond the gas-works.

'Pinch me!' groaned Tom. 'I must be dreaming.'

Now the speck, the spark, dwindled into nothing. It had gone.

'Oh no, it's gone!' wailed Alice. 'Oh, I wanted it! Why's it gone?'

She burst into tears.

THREE

When Tom awoke next morning the first thing he thought of was the great impossible golden cat. It had gone strolling off into the night sky and the whole thing was impossible, but they had seen it with their own eyes, all three of them.

'Unless I was dreaming.'

He sat up. There lay the faded cloth bag on the carpet, where it had dropped after he'd tipped out the bones. The only thing was . . . He got up and went slowly over. He touched it with a finger and felt the hardness. Then he heard the chink, and knew that he was right. 'The cat's back in the bag!'

He couldn't for the life of him think *how*, but then he couldn't work *any* of it out. It was outside the laws of nature, the whole thing. But he was beginning to get used to it.

'Hi there, cat!' he whispered. 'Don't go away!
Just going to get the others!'

Alice was ecstatic when she heard.

'Oh the darling cat! It's back!'

'Don't be soppy,' Tom told her.

'It was ginormous,' Griselda said. 'More like a
baby lion.'

'I'm going to give it some milk, I'm going—'

'No chance,' said Tom. 'It's gone back to
bones again.'

'What?'

''Fraid so.'

They all went to his room and stared down at
the bundle on the carpet.

'Puss!' called Alice. 'Puss puss puss!'

'Idiot!' Tom told her.

Alice seemed to forget she was not keen on bones
and skeletons. She crouched by the bag, pulled at
the cord and peered inside.

'Let's tip them out again!'

'No!' said Griselda.

'Why not?'

'Because it hasn't asked us to. They're not just

any old bones, you know. You can't just go tipping them out and fooling around with them as if they were Lego or something.'

'So what are we supposed to do?' asked Tom. 'Shove 'em back under the bed and wait?'

'All I know is Mum had better not find them,' said Griselda.

She was right, they could see that.

'Leave it for now, then when we've had breakfast we'll decide what to do,' Tom said.

So they went down and had a special half-term breakfast of sausages and beans. Then they went back upstairs, and Mrs Dogberry called after them, 'I hope you're not going to spend all day hunched over that computer!'

'The point is,' Tom said, 'even if it does come to life again, it's risky here. It was different last night.'

'Mum might like it,' Alice said.

'Oh *yeah*!' said Tom. 'And where would we say it'd come from? "Dug it up in the graveyard", or what?'

'Not to mention her asthma,' said Griselda.

'We could say it was a stray.'

'It is, in a way, I suppose,' Griselda said. 'The only thing is it's it's size, it's—'

'It's half the size of a sheep,' Tom said. 'And Mum'd smell a rat the minute she laid eyes on it. Not to mention the amount it must eat. Hey, that's a thought – *does* it eat? I mean, all it really is is a bag of old bones!'

'Don't think I can't hear you,' came a voice. 'Bag of old bones indeed!'

'You're not, you're not!' cried Alice. '*I* don't think you are, I think you're beautiful, and come out puss, please come out!'

'No, don't!' said Griselda swiftly. 'I mean, it's not that I don't want to see you, I do, but not here.'

'We've got this mother, you see,' Tom said.

'Oh, I know about mothers,' said the voice. 'So what *are* you going to do? I much prefer being alive to dead, you know.'

'What if . . .' Griselda had an inspiration. 'What if we took you back to where I found you?'

'Then you could come out and no one else would see you.'

'Oh yes, let's,' said Alice.

'Now we're getting somewhere,' said the voice.

So that is what they did. Mrs Dogberry was pleased that her children were going into the fresh air, and it was easy enough to make sure that she didn't see the bag of bones.

It was such a short way to the park that it was very bad luck indeed for them to meet the Murdoch.

'Oh flip!' muttered Tom. 'Just our luck!'

He was safely out of her class now, but remembered only too well what it was like to be in it.

'Good morning, children!'

'Good morning, Miss Murdoch!' they chorused dutifully.

She had exceedingly sharp eyes. She could spot notes being passed under desks at twenty metres, she could spot telltale smudges of chocolate or crumbs on fingers and lips, so she was certainly not going to miss a rather large old bag. The main reason she spotted it was because she saw that Tom was trying to hide it.

'Whatever have you got there, Tom?' she exclaimed.

'Nothing,' he mumbled, but her skinny hand shot out and snatched at the bag. Tom hung on to it like grim death.

'It's disgusting, it's filthy! And whatever's in it?'

Alice groaned and squeezed her eyes shut. She could hear the bones jingle and clash.

'Does your mother know? Open it this minute!'

'It's nothing,' said Griselda, 'really it's not.'

'Open it, I said. Tom!'

Tom had had years of doing what Miss Murdoch told him. He did it automatically. He pulled apart the drawstring. Miss Murdoch stretched her neck and peered in.

'Eeech!' She let out a long, piercing scream, and Griselda cried, 'Run for it!' and they did, all three of them, leaving the Murdoch to scream at thin air. They did not stop till they were safely inside the park gates, and even then only to draw breath.

'Quick!' gasped Griselda. 'In the bushes.'

None of them had ever seen the Murdoch run, but for all they knew she might. They pushed in among the laurels and flowering currants. The leaves sprang and quivered about them.

'Phew!' Tom let out a long breath.

'It's all right for you, you're not in her class,' Griselda told him.

'It wasn't *you* who had the bag,' Tom pointed out.

'Oh, it'll all be shaken up,' said Alice. 'Will it be hurt?'

'Let me out!' came a plaintive, mewing voice.

'It's not!' said Alice joyfully. 'Let it out, quick!'

So Tom tipped the bag, very gently, and the bones flew out and lay for an instant on the loamy earth. Then, as before, they started to assemble, but this time it was in broad daylight. Even so there seemed to be an extra light, and as the huge cat took shape it seemed to fringe its prodigious furriness like a halo.

'Oh there you are!' Alice was ecstatic.

'You're not hurt, are you?' asked Griselda.

'Now we are back where we started,' said the cat, looking about.

'But *why* are we?' Tom asked. 'I mean, what were you doing here in the first place?'

'You had better ask *her*,' replied the cat, and it fixed Griselda with its yellowy eyes. So did her brother and sister (though their eyes were not yellow, but blue and brown).

'Go on, then,' Tom said. 'Tell us.'

'I . . . I don't know,' she replied truthfully. 'Not exactly. The only thing is . . . well, I did make a wish.'

'Exactly!' said the cat.

'You what? You wished for a bag of old bones?'

'Of course not! I just . . . just wished something exciting would happen.'

'And it did! You're exciting,' Alice told the cat. 'You're the most excitingest thing I've ever seen. But I wish—'

'Careful,' warned the cat.

'So what now?' Tom said.

The cat did not reply. Instead, it turned and began to thread its way further into the bushes. They followed. They seemed to go a long way, they would never have guessed the shrubbery was so deep and dense. Soon the yells and laughter of children in the park had faded, and they heard only the tramping of their own feet. As they went, the bushes grew wilder and thicker, and the ground under their feet was rough and brambly. The park gardeners could not have been digging there for years. It was growing darker, too. If they tilted back their heads they could see tall trees crowding above them and shutting out the sky. But in the dimness the cat was glowing with its own private light. They kept their eyes fixed on its waving tail and followed.

It reached a small clearing and stopped. The children looked up and saw that ahead was the mouth of a cave. The stones were weather-worn and covered in moss, and beyond lay a deep darkness. Alice went forward and peered in and could feel its coldness coming to meet her. 'Ugh! Spooky!'

They had never been in a cave before, and although they had never been forbidden to do so, they were quite sure their mother would not want them to. They each fervently hoped that they would not be asked to.

'Now we are coming to the very edge of the world,' the cat said.

'But the world hasn't got an edge,' objected Tom. 'It's round.'

'To the edge of *this* world,' the cat said. 'Surely you knew there was another?'

'Well, no, actually,' Tom said.

'We haven't done it yet at school,' said Griselda swiftly.

'Oh, you won't have,' said the cat. 'No one will tell you about it. You have to discover it for yourself.'

'Is the other world where you come from?' Alice asked. 'You're not from round here. Cats aren't as big as you round here.'

'So are we going to get a look at this other world, or not?' said Tom impatiently.

'If you wish,' the cat replied. 'But I must make one thing clear. You may look at it. But if you wish to enter it, you must be very brave.'

'I'm not particularly brave,' Alice said. 'I think I'm a bit young to be brave.'

The cat looked at her, and again its mouth seemed to curve into a smile.

'We shall see about that,' it said.

It turned and began to stalk into the cave, and it glowed and lit the rocky floor so that they could see their way. Griselda looked nervously about for bats. She had heard that they flew into people's hair, and she had more than the others. She saw massive boulders, yawning holes and curiously crusted rocks barnacled by time.

The three followed the cat deeper and deeper into the cave. Their footsteps echoed and the air was icy. Then they heard the voice.

'Stop! Don't go!'

The words went running about the cavern and struck its roof. They stopped dead and Alice clutched at Griselda.

'What was that?' she whispered, and her whisper too went running about them like a little hissing snake.

The cat was treading on ahead and its light went with it. If they hung back they would soon be in darkness, and that darkness would be deeper than any they had known before. They had already gone a long way into a world that was so out of the ordinary that you could not imagine it even being a particular day of the week, let alone a time of day or night. They each knew, though they did not say it, that they were in a place where time was counted only in millions of years. There was no Monday, Tuesday or Wednesday, no breakfast or dinner times, only the kind of time that counts when a new star is born or an old one dies.

'Come on!' Tom whispered.

The cat and its light were far ahead now.

'Go back! Go back before it's too late!' The voice was fierce and harsh.

Tom jumped and Griselda and Alice grabbed at one another.

'Back! Back!' The walls of the cave were talking, the roof and floor.

'Oh, come on!' Alice tugged at Griselda, and she looked back and saw that there was still a tiny glimmer of daylight. Tom saw it, too.

'Better run for it!' he said.

And so they did. They turned and ran back from the edge of the world, and as they ran they heard loud laughter, spiteful and cackling. The horrid laughter splintered into a thousand echoes and seemed to come from all directions. Not one of them dared to look and see if there was anyone – or anything – there. They kept their eyes fixed on the daylight ahead and ran for their lives.

At last they ran out of the mouth of the cave and tumbled to the ground in a heap, gasping. It was ages before any of them had enough breath to speak.

'Phew!' Tom gasped at last. 'That was a close thing!'

'Who . . . What was it? That voice and that horrible laughing?'

'But the cat . . .' said Alice. 'What about the cat?'

'It'll be out,' Tom told her. 'Soon as it realises we're not following it.'

He turned to look back into the cave for a sign of the cat. His eyes stretched. 'I don't believe it!'

The others looked, too.

'It's gone! Where's the cave gone?'

Four

When three people see the same impossible thing it becomes trebly impossible. When Griselda had seen that the second hand of her watch had stopped moving, it was something she dared not mention to her brother and sister. Afterwards, she had even wondered if she had imagined it.

But now all three saw that where there had been the yawning entrance to a deep dark cave there were now only bushes.

But these bushes were not part of the dense undergrowth the cat had led them through. They were ordinary park shrubs, properly spaced and tidy. Suddenly they all realised that they could hear voices and the laughter of children playing. They had run back into the real world.

They looked at one another and were secretly ashamed that they had run away at the first sign of danger. They had been warned that they must be brave. They had been following that wonderful shining cat towards a great adventure; they had been almost to the edge of the world – and now it had disappeared, and it served them right.

'Let's go back to the cave,' said Griselda. 'It might not be too late!'

'Go back where?' said Tom. 'That forest it took us through, it's not there. Anyone can see that.'

'But it must be there!' said Alice. 'P'raps if we just start walking we'll find it like we did before.'

'We were following the cat then,' Griselda reminded her.

'Oh the cat, the beautiful pussy-cat! Oh, won't we ever see it again?'

'I don't know,' replied Griselda truthfully.

'Stop snivelling, Alice,' said Tom. He was mad at her because he was mad at himself. As the eldest, he was not proud of run away from what, after all, had only been a voice. Though he had not much liked the sound of that laughter . . .

'So now what?' Griselda felt flat and empty. 'Do you think if we . . .' her voice trailed off. She stared at something lying on the ground by the laurel.

It was there again, that faded cloth bag, exactly as when she had first found it.

'Oh hurray!' Alice ran to it and dropped to her knees. 'Are you there? Puss puss puss!'

Griselda joined her. 'Please, cat, come out! We're sorry we ran, we really are!'

The bag lay floppy and dumb. But the bones were there all right. That amazing furry cat was actually in there, somehow.

'Look,' said Tom, 'we've said we're sorry. We honestly are. Please come out again.'

They waited. The bag did not stir. They heard only far-off voices and the whistle of birds.

'Shall we tip it out?' Alice whispered.

'No!' said Griselda.

'Why not?'

'I told you before. It hasn't asked us to.'

'So what shall we do then?'

'Wait. Tell it we're sorry again.'

So they did. They each said sorry twenty times. They begged and pleaded, but all in vain. The bag lay obstinately still and silent.

'I give up,' Tom said. 'Might as well go home.'

'We can't give up!' said Griselda desperately. 'It'll

think we don't care, and then we might never see it again!'

'We'll take the bag with us. Then we can keep having another go.'

There seemed nothing else they could do. So Tom picked up the bag and they went home, keeping a sharp eye out for the Murdoch.

The minute they were through the door their mother was there, and her eyes went straight to the bag Tom was trying to hide.

'So it was true! I simply couldn't believe my ears when she told me. Give that to me this minute.'

The girls watched in anguish as Tom slowly drew his arm from behind his back and held out the bag.

'It's not what you think!' cried Alice. 'It's not really bones, it's a— Ouch!'

Griselda had kicked her, hard. Something warned her that the golden cat was not to be spoken of, that it was a secret meant only for the three of them.

'Ugh! Just what she said: horrible old bones! I'm surprised at you, I really am!'

The trio stood dumb, their eyes fixed on the precious bag.

'Well, there's only one place for this!'

She marched past them and into the yard, raised the dustbin lid and they winced as they heard the bones clash and rattle. *Bang!* Down went the lid. The cat was trapped, and lying in a jumble of empty tins, potato peelings and cabbage stalks.

'There!' exclaimed Mrs Dogberry. 'That's where that belongs! And there's a funny thing—'

'What?'

'Such a funny thing. Just after Miss Murdoch called there was a rag-and-bone-man at the door.'

'A what?'

'I haven't seen one of those for years. I didn't think there were such things any more. A real old-fashioned one, with a push cart!'

'Nobody's *got* any rags or bones,' said Griselda.

'Not many bones in fish-fingers,' Tom said. 'Or burgers.'

'I know, that's what's so funny. And it was bones he was after especially, he said. Kept asking if I was sure there weren't any. Said he'd got a nose for bones.'

The children did not much like the sound of this.

'He won't come back, will he?' asked Alice nervously. She had already made up her mind that they would rescue the bag from the bin, no matter what.

'Whyever should he? Now go along and wash your hands, all of you. And wash them properly. Old bones – ugh!'

They tramped upstairs and noisily washed their hands, talking in low voices.

'We'll have to get it out!' said Griselda.

'Course we will,' Tom agreed. 'First chance we get.'

'That Murdoch's a mean old toad!' said Alice.

'Wait till you're in her *class*!' Griselda told her.

They laid their plans to rescue the bag. Griselda and Alice would distract their mother while Tom raided the bin. Then he would run to the park and put the bag back under the laurel.

'But push it right under,' Alice begged. 'Don't leave it where just anyone could find it.' She was thinking of the mysterious visitor with a nose for bones.

'And tell it we'll be back, we're not just dumping it!' said Griselda. She thought the cat might be in

58

a huff, having been chucked in a dustbin. It must already have been displeased by the three of them running off in the cave.

Tom went downstairs. The girls got out their paints and stirred brushfuls into a jar of water, till it was a good muddy colour.

'OK. That'll do,' decided Griselda, and she tipped the jar over. The khaki mixture spread on the carpet in a dark stain. Alice shrieked, and she was not entirely acting. 'Mum, Mum! Quick!'

As soon as Mrs Dogberry started up the stairs Tom made for the bin. He yanked out the bag, brushed off the bits of rubbish, and ran.

'Sorry!' he said. 'Not our fault, you know!' and he was on the street in a flash.

'Raggabow! Raggabow!' A man's voice was calling. Ahead, Tom saw someone pushing a handbarrow.

'Raggabow! Raggabow!' The man was between Tom and the park gates. Tom could have hidden and waited for the man to go by. But he had already been a coward once today, and did not believe that very much could happen in broad daylight on his own street. He simply held the bag as close to his side as possible, and slowed to a casual saunter.

He drew level with the cart. It was a shock when suddenly his way was blocked.

'Well then, young sir!' The man himself was a bundle of rags and bones. His eyes glittered in his grimed face and his teeth gleamed yellow. 'Bones I'm after, and bones is what you've got!'

His eyes were fixed on the bag. Tom clutched it tightly.

'Go away!' he said.

'Oh no,' said the man. 'Oh no. Not till I've got what I'm after!'

'I – I haven't got anything.'

'Hand 'em over, better,' said the man. 'Kids' mothers don't like 'em messing about with bones. Especial the particular bones you got there.'

'It's – it's none of your business!' said Tom.

All at once the man made a grab at the bag. Tom sidestepped swiftly and darted off. His mind was working fast, and when he reached the park gates he did not go in, but kept running.

''Ere, you! Stop!'

Tom did not stop. He ran and ran and of course

the bones clanked and clattered, and he muttered, 'Sorry, sorry, sorry!', and hoped the cat would hear and understand. He could not think how it felt to be a jumble of bones being shaken, but imagined it was not much fun. He did not stop till he reached the main road and the shops, and felt he was safe. Ahead of him was another entrance to the park. Soon the cat would be safely back under the laurel.

Back at number 27 Lime Street, the girls were busy mopping up the spill.

'I expect the stain will come out,' said Griselda, who had certainly believed this when she'd tipped over the jar.

'I just hope so,' her mother said. 'I'm beginning to wish half-term was over already. First bones, now this.'

Griselda and Alice looked at one another and fervently hoped that she would not realise that the two incidents were connected.

'Tom must be there by now!' whispered Alice, as soon as their mother went back down.

'Ssshh! What's that?'

'Raggabow! Raggabow!'

Griselda ran to the window, pushed up the sash and stuck her head out. 'That man! The one Mum told us about!'

Alice peered out past her. 'Oh no! The one who can sniff bones!'

'Raggabow! Raggabow!'

The man was outside their house now, and all at once he lifted his head and was looking straight at them. In that instant they both had the queerest feeling that they knew him, had seen him before somewhere. It had always struck Griselda as amazing that all human beings have the same features – eyes, nose, mouth, chin – yet not two of them ever look exactly the same (not counting identical twins, of course). They did not know anyone half as dirty as this man, or with such yellowy teeth as he leered up at them, yet they knew him.

'Bones?' he whined. 'Any bones?'

'No!' said Griselda, and she pushed Alice back and slammed the window down. Her heart hammered. Alice whispered, 'What if he knocks on the door again? What if he asks Mum?'

The words were no sooner out than *ratatat*, the knocker was rapped hard. The pair clutched at one another and held their breath. They heard their mother go to the door and open it.

'Now we're for it!'

But Griselda was wrong. They heard their mother speak sharply and – *bang*! The door shut. Then she came up the stairs, grumbling to herself.

'Pest. Bones indeed! Whatever for, I'd like to know. There's no one rummaging in *my* bin for bones. Have you got that mark out yet?'

The girls smiled at her so radiantly that she was startled.

'Oh yes,' Griselda assured her. 'Look, you won't notice a thing once it's dry.'

'Look out the window and you'll see that man and his cart I told you about. You'll probably never see another.'

So Alice and Griselda went unwillingly and looked down and their mother looked, too, because even she seemed to feel there was something fishy going on. And, as if the man could feel their eyes upon him, he turned and looked up. His face twisted and he shook a fist.

'Well!' exclaimed Mrs Dogberry. 'What a horrible man. I've a good mind to ring the police.'

'Oh, don't!' said Alice and Griselda together.

She gave them both a hard look.

'You're up to something,' she said. 'I can tell.' And went out.

'She doesn't know *what*, though,' said Alice when their mother had gone. 'And she couldn't possibly guess, never in a million years. What's *happening*, Grizzles?'

'I don't know,' replied Griselda truthfully. 'But Alice . . . did that man remind you of anyone?'

'Well, yes. But it can't have—'

'Who?'

Griselda already guessed the answer.

'Well . . . the Murdoch!'

'Me, too!'

'Could it be her brother, d'you think?' asked Alice.

'Well it can't exactly have been her in disguise,' Griselda said. 'You know what she's like. Always sending notes to people's mothers if their trainers are dirty, and sending them out to wash their hands. She'd have a blue fit at anyone like that!'

'It's queer, though,' said Alice.

Griselda agreed that it was. 'I wonder if Tom saw him,' she said.

'Where is Tom?' asked Alice. 'He should be back by now. There's an awful lot happening, isn't there? I'm beginning to get wobbles in my tummy.'

'Well don't!' Griselda told her sternly.

Alice was very prone to what she called 'wobbles in my tummy'. Sometimes she went quite white and shaky, sometimes she was even sick. Mrs Dogberry said this was because she was 'highly strung'. Her brother and sister said it was because she was just plain wet.

'Daft mump!' Tom would say. (No one knew why he called people this, he just did. He had since he was tiny, Mrs Dogberry said.)

Griselda was more charitable, but even she would become impatient if Alice showed signs of wobbly tummy at important times, like going on holiday or a trip to London.

'Just try taking deep breaths,' she would advise.

She always read the magazines in the doctor's and dentist's waiting-rooms, and often picked up useful tips from them. She already knew quite a lot about what you should or should not do when you were expecting a baby.

Alice stood and took several loud and noisy breaths, concentrating so hard that her face went pink.

'That's better,' Griselda told her approvingly. 'But you're right, you know. Tom should be back by now. And he's got the bag of bones.'

'And that horrible Raggabow's after them, I'm sure he is!'

'So am I,' said Griselda. So we'd better think what we're going to do. Fast.'

FIVE

T om sat cross-legged in the shrubbery, staring
hard at the bag of bones. He was willing it
to move. He too read magazines in waiting-rooms,
and knew that such a thing was possible, if he tried
hard enough. He had not really believed it at the
time he read it, but it suited him to believe it now.
The cat – if it was still in there – was obviously in
a deep sulk, and might never come out of the bag
again of its own accord.

Tom stared unwinkingly, willing the bones
to move. He stared so hard that his eyes
began to water. And he thought the thought
I will you to move, I will you to move so
many times and so hard that his brain began
to ache.

'I give up!' he said at last.

He tried another plan.

'Listen, cat,' he said, 'we're all dead sorry we ran

off out of the cave like that. We're sorrier than we've ever been in our whole lives.'

He waited for some sign, but none came.

'And it was terrible, Mum chucking you in the dustbin,' he went on. 'And I know it was our fault we ran off in the cave, but *that* wasn't our fault. It was that rotten Murdoch. It was her that dobbed on us. She can't stand kids and she can't stand 'em having any fun. Can't think why she was a teacher in the first place. Witch, more like.'

The bag lay slumped and lifeless. The cat might not even have been listening.

'I'm not going to leave you here, you know,' Tom said, though for all he knew he was talking to thin air. 'Not now. No fear. That Raggabow's after you. In fact you ought to be grateful to me – just a bit grateful, anyhow. He'd have grabbed you if I hadn't run for it.'

The bag showed not the least sign of gratitude. Tom was beginning to feel desperate. The plan had been for him to conceal the bag under the laurel and go back home. He now began to wish that the plan had been for the girls to join him. He could be sitting here for ever – for hours and hours, at any rate. He decided to try telepathy, which he had also read about in a magazine. It seemed far-fetched, but it was worth a try. He shut his eyes and pictured his sisters back home, and sent them a thought as strongly as he knew how: *Come to the park, come to the park, come to the park*!

The trouble was, he wouldn't know whether it was working or not. He looked at his watch.

'I'll give 'em ten minutes,' he decided.

Those minutes passed very slowly. They seemed to stretch into ten hours.

'They're not coming, cat,' he said. 'So now what?'

'Actions speak louder than words!' The voice came from the bag of bones.

'You *are* there!' exclaimed Tom. 'Yippee! Er – what d'you mean, exactly?'

He waited but there was no reply.

'Puss puss puss. Come on, puss!' He knew that he sounded as soppy as Alice, and was glad there was no one to hear him.

When he realised that there was to be no answer, Tom started to think about what the bones had said: 'Actions speak louder than words.'

He'd heard it said before, always by grown-ups. You didn't catch kids saying things like that. He thought he knew what it meant vaguely, but now he tried to work out exactly what the cat was trying to tell him. He thought for quite a long time. Then he stood up.

'OK,' he said. 'I think I get it. We've *said* sorry for running off in the cave, we've said it about a million times. If you don't believe us, I'll show you. I'm going to see if I can find that cave again. Now.'

He paused, half hoping for an answer.

'I'll have to take you with me. Not safe here, what with Raggabow and the Murdoch.'

He picked up the bag and started to push his way through the bushes. It was ordinary park shrubbery, he knew that. But he also believed that beyond it lay a dark forest and a gaping cave. He had been there. He didn't particularly want to go there on his own, but if there was any chance that it would please the cat, he would do it.

'He's not here!'

'Nor's the bag!'

Tom had never before been so glad to hear his sisters' voices.

'I'm here!'

He turned back.

'Why were you hiding?' demanded Alice.

'There's this horrible man with a cart!'

'Tell me about it!' said Tom with feeling.

They exchanged stories.

'So what do we do now?' Tom asked. 'We daren't take the bag home and we daren't leave it here.'

'We *dare* take it home, then!' said Alice. 'We got this brill idea, Grizzles and me.'

She triumphantly produced the tote bag she took when she went swimming or to the library.

'All we do is put the cat's bag inside this one,' Griselda said. 'Simple.'

'Good thinking,' Tom said. 'Thought I'd be stuck here for ever.'

'Where were you going when we got here?' Alice asked.

He told her.

'So let's do it,' he said. 'All of us.'

'It's worth a try, I suppose,' Griselda agreed.

'But what if we *do* find the forest, and then get lost,' said Alice. 'Are you sure the cat won't come out? Puss! Puss puss puss!'

'Drop it, Alice,' Tom told her. 'It's useless. Come on. If I dared do it on my own, you ought to dare when there's three of us.'

So they did. Tom led the way and they pushed through the springing branches and there they were under an ordinary sky; and then, from one moment to the next, there was a strange shift and the world darkened and they were back in the forest. Tom stopped.

'It worked!' he whispered.

They stood gazing fearfully about them and upwards, to where the branches crowded out the sky. The trees were ancient, their trunks carved with whorls and spirals like fossils.

'There aren't any birds,' Alice whispered.

The wood was eerily silent. It was the deepest silence they had ever known.

'Let me out! Let me out!'

'Oh cat,' said Alice joyfully. 'You *are* still there!'

Tom pulled the cord and gently tipped the bones on to the mossy ground. They all watched as the bones began their slow, amazing dance. They watched intently, hardly daring to blink in case they missed the actual moment when the cat came in all its dense furriness. There it was, melting out of the air. It stood glowing in the greenish light, and its golden eyes were reproachful.

'You ran away,' it said.

'We know. We were idiots,' Tom said.

'And we never will again,' Griselda promised.

'Are we – are we going back to that cave?' asked Alice nervously.

'It's up to you,' replied the cat. 'If you like I can disappear and you'll never set eyes on me again.'

'Oh no!' all three said instantly.

'Then you had better follow me,' it said. 'But I've warned you before and I'll warn you again, we're going right to the edge of the world.'

'Right,' said Tom. 'Fine. That's OK by me.' And he gave Alice a warning look. This was no time for anyone to spring a wobbly tummy. He picked up the empty bag and stuffed it into the tote bag.

'Ready!' he said.

So the cat led the way and they followed its glowing form. As before, the forest grew deeper and denser. The only sound was the soft scuff of their feet. It was easy to believe they were making their way towards the very edge of the world. And it was hard to tell how long it was before they found themselves at the mouth of the cave again.

The cat went treading on without a pause and its fringe of light shone more brightly in the gloom.

'Come on,' said Tom. 'And remember: don't run!'

'Whatever happens,' added Griselda.

'Whatever happens,' repeated Alice in a wobbly voice, and she clutched at her sister's hand.

The second journey into the cave was more scary than the first. Because they had heard that harsh voice and spiteful laughter they peered harder into every crevice, and looked more often over their shoulders. They kept steadily on because the glow of the cat was the only light they had.

'Look out! Go back!' They were half expecting the voice, but when it came they all jumped.

'Go back! Go back!' The echoes ran about them.

'Go back yourself!' shouted Tom, and with delight heard his own voice multiply into echoes.

'Go back!'

'Shan't!' cried Griselda, and her voice too split and overlapped the other.

Back . . . back . . . back . . .

Alice plucked up courage.

'You go away!' she shouted.

Now all the echoes were mingling.

'You want a shouting match, you've got one!' called Tom. 'Come on, all shout!'

So they did, and their voices bounced from the walls and roof, and the echoes criss-crossed so that you did not hear the separate words at all, only a kind of mad chorus. And the madder it got, the more the children liked it. They swung their arms and marched after the cat, yelling whatever came into their heads to drown that voice. Alice sang 'Heigh-ho, heigh-ho, it's off to work we go', like the seven dwarfs, and it hardly mattered at all when she ran out of words, she just kept singing the same ones, over and over.

By the time they realised that the cat had stopped and was waiting for them, their ears were ringing and they felt dizzy and light-headed. The cat was standing by a large, jagged hole in the floor of the cave. The strange thing was that the hole was not dark, but light.

'Now you are here,' the cat said. 'At the rim of the world.'

'Is *that* the edge of the world?' Alice pointed at the hole. 'We won't fall off, will we?'

'Oh, I hope so,' said the cat surprisingly. 'It depends whether you have the nerve. Come and look.'

They went rather slowly, and stood well away from the edge of the hole. They peered down. It was as if they were up in the sky and looking down at another world. Away down below was a kind of rocky valley, a lunar landscape.

'Wow!' muttered Tom. 'It's not the moon, is it? Can't be!'

'Oh it could,' the cat assured him. 'It could be anything.'

First they took in the strange volcanic rocks and rough stone pillars.

'Like Stonehenge,' whispered Alice, who had never visited that mysterious place, but had seen pictures.

Then, as their eyes grew accustomed to the light, they noticed something else.

'Bones!' gasped Griselda. 'Millions and millions of bones!'

They lay strewn at random, all shapes and sizes, as far as the eye could see. The children had hardly ever seen a real bone, except now and then at the butcher's in the High Street. Now they were gazing down at a world littered with them. All they could see were rocks and stones and bones. There was not even a hint of green, just a landscape that could have been carved out of ice, pale and fantastic.

'You don't – you don't think this is where Raggabow lives?' whispered Alice.

'Nobody lives here,' said Tom. 'Everything – everyone's – dead.'

'You are in the sky and looking down at another world,' the cat said.

'In the sky?' repeated Alice. 'We're in the sky?'

'In a manner of speaking,' the cat said. 'What do you think of the view?'

None of them knew what to say.

'Er – it's very interesting,' said Tom at last. 'Whose are all those bones?'

'That is for you to find out,' the cat replied. 'Shall we go down?'

'But, there aren't any stairs!' Alice drew back from the edge of the hole.

'I told you, we're up in the sky,' the cat said.

'That's that, then,' said Tom. 'We can't exactly jump.'

'Oh you can,' the cat said. 'If you dare!'

'Jump?' Griselda was horrified. 'We'd break every bone in our bodies!'

'Probably how those bones got there in the first place,' Tom muttered. 'No thanks.'

'What about you?' The cat fixed Griselda with its yellow eyes. 'Or are you as cowardly as your brother?'

'I'd like to,' she said. 'Honestly. But the thing is . . . we can't fly. Not like you.'

'How do you know until you try?' the cat asked. 'Can you swim?'

'Yes!' replied all three in chorus.

'There you are, then. If you can swim, you can fly. All it takes is a little nerve. Follow me!'

The cat sprang. They gasped. It brushed past them

and was suddenly there below them, treading air. It hovered with its plumy tail up like a rudder.

'Wow! I don't believe it! P'raps it *is* the moon! No gravity.'

'There must be some,' said Griselda. 'Look, it's going down.'

The cat was slowly descending, but paddling air, not as if pulled by the huge force of gravity. Then it rolled over on to its back – its great paws waving – and looked up at them.

'Are you coming?' it called.

Griselda made up her mind.

'I am!' She swung her legs over the edge, took a deep breath and launched herself.

She shut her eyes as she jumped, but knew almost at once that she could open them again. She was flying! She had spread her arms like wings, but she didn't need to, because what she was doing was more like swimming – swimming in air. And just as you are buoyed up by water, so she seemed to be held by the air. Nearby she saw the cat, still rolling with its paws waving, and she could hear it purr as if it were on a favourite lap.

'Grizzles!' She looked up and saw the faces of

her brother and sister peering over the edge of the hole, their eyes popping.

'Come on,' she called. 'It's ace! Brilliant! Fantabulous!'

'Coming,' shouted Tom, then 'wow!' as he jumped and found himself floating. 'Woweeee!'

'And me . . . Oh dear! Oh! Oh!' Alice took the plunge, she curled herself into a ball and rolled over the edge and squealed as she went. But once she found herself safe and floating, she stuck out her arms and legs like a starfish, and beamed from ear to ear.

'I'm doing the crawl,' Tom shouted. 'Watch me!'

They experimented, all three of them, with this new element.

'Like swimming, only easier!' Griselda spun herself round like a weather vane.

'And if you want to go down, you just do this!' Tom had already worked out what to do by watching the cat. You stood upright and made fast little treading motions on the spot.

'I don't want to go down! I want to stop here for ever!'

If they landed, it was going to be difficult to avoid treading on bones. And bones are dead people or animals. Alice paddled over to where the cat still lay on its back, with its eyes shut and a blissful smile. Cats always look as if they are smiling, but she felt sure this one actually was. She scrabbled her fingers in the dense fur and its purr deepened to a growl.

'O pussy, O pussy, O pussy my love, what a beautiful pussy you are you are, what a beautiful pussy you are!'

The cat winked through half-shut eyes.

'Look, this is how you go up!'

Tom had his arms stretched right up, and was clawing at air like a tiger in slow motion.

Griselda copied him and found herself ascending, too.

'Not too high,' came Alice's voice. 'Look out, or you'll hit the roof!'

Griselda had forgotten that this strange sky they were in did not stretch up for ever like the one in their own world. She had already reached the floor of the cave, and touched it with her fingertips before treading her feet to go down again. She looked down and saw that the cat had rolled the right way up again and was treading its paws to go down. Down and down it went, until at last it reached the ground, and there was a great marmalade splash among all those whitened bones.

The children paddled air towards one another till they were bobbing in a cluster.

'Must we go down?' said Alice.

'I think it wants us to.' Griselda too would rather have stayed in the air.

'Don't fancy it much,' Tom said. 'Hey, what if all those other bones are really cats?'

'And what if we could make them all come alive?' added Alice.

'Don't *look* much like cats.' Griselda peered down. 'Not some of them, anyway. More like—'

She stopped. Some of the bones were as long as tree trunks, some of the skulls could easily be those of elephants, or even dinosaurs.

'Are you coming or not?' The cat was watching them, daring them.

'Better, I s'pose,' Tom said. 'Here goes!'

Six

T om trod air furiously, and the others followed suit and next minute they were down. Each took care to land on a space between the bones. They looked about at the deserted valley and realised that again there was utter silence, as if the world was holding its breath.

In any ordinary place they would have started to explore, but here none of them felt like taking a single step. To do so would mean treading on a skeleton.

'Why are we here?' asked Griselda at last.

'To make something happen,' the cat replied.

'Er – make what happen?' Tom asked.

'Anything,' the cat said. 'There's nothing happening at the moment, you can see that for yourself.'

The three exchanged looks and wished that the cat did not talk in riddles.

'Of course, you can just stand here for ever, if you like,' it said.

'But we don't know what to do,' said Alice. 'I don't like it here, I want to go home!'

'She doesn't!' said Griselda swiftly. 'None of us do!'

'But at this rate we *shall* stand here for ever,' said Tom.

The cat yawned so that they could see down its pink throat. 'Suit yourselves,' it said, and turned its back. For a moment it stood, then set off among the jumbled bones as if searching for something. It stopped, then put out a paw and dabbed.

It happened too quickly for them to see how. A mouse was all at once there and scampering, and the cat was after it.

'See that? A live mouse!'

All three looked down about their feet. Where there is one mouse, there are usually more.

'It's caught it!'

The cat was shaking its head from side to side.

'That's the worst thing about cats,' said Griselda. 'Why can't they be satisfied with things out of tins?'

'The point is,' said Tom slowly, 'it's not quite so dead around here as we thought.'

'Don't keep talking about dead!' pleaded Alice.

'Girls!' said Tom.

'Boys!' said Griselda.

The cat turned and made its way back to where they stood. It was bright and gingery among all the grey and white, and the only moving thing in the valley. It stopped, then bent its head and seemed to be searching, perhaps for another mouse. Then it deliberately put out a paw and dabbed.

This time they saw what happened. A bird flew up as if startled. But it was newly born, they knew that. A moment before it had not existed. It had hatched out of a bone at the touch of the cat's paw. They saw the blue flash of its wings.

'It's a kingfisher!'

The cat crouched, tail twitching.

'Oh it mustn't, it mustn't! Poor bird! If only there were some trees.'

The words were no sooner out of Alice's mouth than there was a huge greening. In front of them trees sprang up with a shiver of leaves. They rose smoothly up and were centuries old in the twinkling of an eye. Both cat and bird had vanished from sight.

They stared dumbstruck at the wall of green. Alice clutched at Griselda's hand. She had hated the bare rocky valley, but now she was frightened by the sudden green. What was worse, she had the feeling that she herself had made it happen.

'Cat!' she called. 'Puss, puss!'

'I don't believe this,' Tom said. 'What happened?'

'It's gone green,' said Griselda. 'But – but the bones are still there.'

They shuffled closer together, staring down at the skulls and knuckles. They had just seen a kingfisher hatch out of one. That was harmless enough. But who knew what lay sleeping in some of the larger ones?

The cat appeared out of the trees. Mercifully, it was not licking its lips. 'I see you are beginning to get the idea,' it said. 'Now, take your pick!'

'If you mean what I think you mean, I'm not sure I want to,' Tom said.

'I do!' said Griselda. 'Cat, you know when you

made that mouse come, and that bird . . .? How did you know which bone to touch?'

'Oh, it's easier than you think,' the cat replied. 'Try.'

Griselda did not wish to produce a wolf, or a tiger. She preferred something more harmless. She was wondering what, exactly, when an old rhyme came into her head.

That would do! she thought.

She stepped forward, knelt, and looked for a suitable bone.

'Careful, Grizzles!' cried Alice. 'Oh, I think my tummy's going wobbly!'

'Daft mump!' Tom told her. 'Shut up and watch.'

Griselda, feeling enormously brave and strong, put out a finger and touched, ever so gently, the chosen bone. It was as if her own finger was a magic wand. She touched, and felt fleetingly the cold hardness, and the next moment there was warm softness. She snatched back her hand and found herself staring into a leathery black face with small black and yellow eyes.

Baa, baa, black sheep, have you any wool . . . 'It worked!' she gasped.

'Hurray!' yelled Alice.

'Baaa!' bleated the sheep.

'It's crazy!' Tom was jumping up and down. 'I want to do it!'

'Careful,' warned Griselda, proud of her black sheep. She couldn't get over it. She had made it, or as good as. The cat walked over to inspect and stood gazing up as if it were a ginger lamb.

'Very good,' it said. 'As a start, I suppose. What are you going to do with it?'

'*Do* with it?' Griselda was startled. She had no idea what you did with sheep.

'You chose it,' the cat told her. 'I think it's rather tame, myself. Look at it. All it does is chew.'

They all looked. The sheep gazed mildly back and chewed.

'It's true, Grizzles,' Tom said. 'Boring. Here, let me have a go!'

He already had his eye on a huge, ribby spine, and half hoped he knew what it might turn into. He didn't really think what he was doing. His school reports always said, *Tom must stop and think before rushing into things. He is in too much of a hurry*. Which is another way of saying, 'Look before you leap.'

Tom touched the bone and – *whoosh*! He shrank back cowering with his arms shielding his face, and heard his sisters' screams and the sheep's startled bleat.

'Quick! Run!' Griselda was pulling at his arm, and all three of them ran into the trees. The sheep scampered ahead on its silly thin legs. They felt heat scorching on their backs. Once in the cool safety of the trees, they stopped and turned.

'Now look what you've gone and done, you silly Tom!' Alice squealed.

It was green and scaly and probably half as long as Lime Street – certainly as long as an Intercity train. Its eyes were like a frog's, only fifty times bigger, and they swivelled alarmingly as if scanning before, behind and sideways all at once. It seemed probable that it could even see its own tail. Like all the best dragons, it was breathing fire.

'Oh help!' said Tom faintly.

The dragon bent its head and snuffed mightily. Then it moved towards them in a long, heavy slither.

'It knows we're here,' whispered Alice. 'It's after us!'

The dragon threw back its head and roared. Flames shot from its long throat and leaves on a nearby tree shrivelled and turned to ash. It seemed to the terrified children that it meant to barbecue them before it ate them, because it had almost certainly got their scent and the sheep's, and had them on its menu. No one ever heard of a vegetarian dragon.

It was only then that they noticed the cat. It had not, as they had supposed, run for cover into the trees with the rest of them. It was padding alongside the dragon and peering up, as if inspecting it, just as it had the sheep. It looked as if it had not a care in the world.

'Cat, quick! Look out!' Alice screamed.

She forgot that they were hiding and that their own lives were at stake. She forgot everything but the amazing cat with its fringe of light that had brought them there and shown them how to fly, and was now about to be reduced to a heap of ashes.

'Cat! Cat!'

'No!' hissed Griselda. 'Look!'

The cat was walking in the path of the dragon and it was walking through the shocking flames with plumed tail and waving whiskers.

'It ought to be dead!' said Tom in shocked tones. He had had enough impossibility for one day.

'P'raps *we* could go through fire!' But even as Griselda spoke, the dragon directed a spear of flame towards the copse where they crouched. They heard the sizzle of the green leaves, saw them blacken and fall.

'It's on to us!'

'Run for it!'

They turned and ran, weaving between the trees, and the sheep ran with them, bleating shrilly. Behind them they heard a great roar, and then the crash and splinter of wood as the dragon entered the forest in pursuit. On they ran and all the while the crashing and splintering grew louder.

'It's catching up'

Tom stopped dead.

'I know what! Fly!'

He put his palms together above his head and pushed with the balls of his feet. He began to rise.

'Hurray!' cried Alice and followed suit.

'But what about my sheep?' It was Griselda's own, and now it would end up as roast mutton.

'Oh – help!'

She looked up and saw that Tom was entangled in the boughs of a tree. He kicked and fought but could go no higher. Alice joined him and she too was stuck. She lay along a thick branch and called, 'Come on, Griselda – quick! It mightn't see us up here!'

Griselda hesitated. There came a roar and a hiss and she thought the air grew warmer. She gave the black sheep a push.

'Run,' she commanded. 'Run – or you'll end up as mutton!'

Then she too made praying hands above her head and pushed up. For a few seconds she was gloriously soaring, and then she was wedged in the tree with the others. She looked down and saw that the sheep had gone.

'Oh, thank goodness!' She could not have borne to see it grilled under her very eyes.

'Are we high enough, d'you think?' asked Tom. 'If the brute looks up and sees us, we're done for!'

It was true. And if the dragon's eyes could swivel before, behind and sideways, there was no reason why they should not swivel upwards, too.

'Hide!' commanded Griselda, and she scrambled higher above a leafy spray, and heard the others scuffling as they did the same. They were just in time.

There was a series of loud crashes, followed by a slither, and their tree rocked and shuddered to its roots. The dragon was right below them. They shut their eyes and held their breath. Then they heard it pant and snort, and thought they felt the warmth of its breath, and could certainly smell burning. It stayed for such an age that Griselda was tempted to part the leaves and look down to see what it was doing. She resisted. If she could see the dragon, it would almost certainly be able to see her.

Then at last there came a muttering roar and the children winced as a wave of heat ran past them. This was followed by a crashing, as (they guessed and hoped) the dragon turned its long length around, cheated of its prey.

Sure enough, the sounds grew fainter, and at last they dared lift their heads and let out their breath.

'Phew! That was a near thing.'

'Has it really gone?'

'Now what?'

The immediate danger had gone, but they were still trapped in a wood so dense that there was no hope of flying free.

'In any case, we'll be miles away from where we came from,' Griselda pointed out. 'We might never find the opening back to the cave. It was only small.'

And the dragon lay between them and the open valley of bones. One by one they let go of their branches and floated back to earth.

'Oh, where's the cat?' cried Griselda desperately.

'The beastly thing's dropped us in it good and proper!' said Tom.

'Don't *call* it that!' said Alice hotly. 'It's lovely. It was you that made the dragon.'

They saw the wide, scorched trail the dragon had left.

'At least we know the way back out,' Tom said. 'We just follow that.'

'Oh yes – and end up practically under its nose!'

'Dragons don't have noses,' he told her. 'Just nostrils. And it's our only chance. For all we know, by the time we get out of here it'll have gone.'

And so they made their way back, climbing over felled trees and gazing with awe and dread at the blackened foliage. At last they glimpsed daylight ahead.

'Now listen,' Tom said. 'As soon as we're clear of the trees, fly!'

'But what if its flames can shoot up miles and miles?' wailed Alice.

They could be fried in midair.

'Well, we'll just have to wait till it goes to sleep, or goes away.'

'For all you know dragons don't go to sleep,' said Alice. 'And even if they do, they might keep one eye open.'

She thought of the huge, rolling eye under its leathery lid, and shuddered.

'I suppose you've got a better idea!' Tom said.

And in that moment Alice did have an idea.

'As a matter of fact, I have,' she said. 'But I'm not telling.'

'Girls!' he said scornfully, and 'Boys!' supplied Griselda.

They moved on, cautiously now, wincing at every snapped twig. For all they knew, the dragon's ears could be as all-hearing as his eyes were all-seeing.

'Better get off the trail now,' Tom whispered. 'It's too open, it'll see us coming.'

So they pushed their way back into the live green foliage and crept towards the daylight. They were right at the very edge of the wood before they could see the rocky ground beyond, and the dragon lying curled as if asleep – or waiting.

'Are its eyes properly shut?' whispered Alice.

It was hard to tell. The huge leathery lids had drooped over those fearsome eyeballs, but who could tell whether there was a narrow slit? All three of them had at one time or another discovered that you could pretend to have your eyes shut, yet be able to see just the same.

'We'll have to risk it,' Tom whispered. 'It's the only way. Just tiptoe out – then, push up for all you're worth!'

'Where's the hole?' asked Griselda, anxiously scanning the white, roofed sky.

'There!' Tom pointed. 'Just above that pillar thing.'

'Oh, where's the cat?'

'Right. Remember: once you're up, go up for all you're worth! You listening, Alice?'

She did not seem to be. She was looking not at the motionless dragon, but at the nearby ribs and knuckles and skulls.

'*Alice!*'

If ever there was a time to develop wobbles in the tummy, this was it. But she actually smiled and nodded. 'Ready!'

They inched forward cautiously. They were playing Grandmother's Footsteps for real. They took a first step into the open and—

Whooosh!

The dragon was awake! It lumbered heavily up, and as it did so Alice snatched a bone and screamed 'Up! Go up!' She threw the bone with all her might towards the dragon. 'Help! Help!'

The bone fell and Alice pointed her fingers above her head for the upward dive and in the same moment, with a flashing of white bones, there sprang up a knight in full armour with blade and lance.

'St George!' screamed Alice, as she rose.

And so it was that the three young Dogberrys had an aerial view of St George slaying the dragon. It was a fight worth seeing. They yelled and clapped and cheered as the knight laid into the dragon and steam rose from its wounds. It writhed and roared, but the knight laid about it until its fire was a mere candle flicker. Aiming his lance, St George pitched it right down the dragon's yawning throat. It gave a last anguished bellow, its tail thrashed and bones flew. Then it sank down and was still.

'Hurray!'

'Three million cheers for St George!'

The knight looked up at the flying children and raised his sword in salute. He looked no more surprised than if they had been starlings.

'Don't I wish I'd got my camera!' Tom said.

'Who did it, who did it? *I* did!' Alice turned a somersault in air.

'What a clever girl, then!' said Griselda.

'For once,' added Tom, who wished he had thought of it himself.

'Oh, I want to go down again!' said Alice. 'All those millions of lovely bones, and they could be *anything*!'

'We know that,' Tom told her. 'Like dragons, for instance. It nearly had us, remember?'

'And whose dragon was it?' asked Griselda.

'At least it was better than a silly sheep!'

They were well on their way to a quarrel.

'Oh stop it!' Alice said. 'Oh – and where's the cat?'

No one knew. They had last seen it walking impossibly through the flames of the dragon's breath.

'What if . . . What if it was frizzled?'

'No chance,' said Tom. But he sounded more certain than he felt.

'Perhaps it's gone back into the bag like it did before,' suggested Griselda. Then, 'Where *is* the bag?'

There was a long silence. For the moment, no one could remember. They trod air and racked their brains.

'You,' said Alice at last to Tom, 'You had it last!'

'So – where is it?' Griselda asked.

Tom honestly could not remember. He did remember picking it up and stuffing it into Alice's tote bag. But that was before they had entered the cave. Had he dropped it before launching himself into air? Or had he still had it when they landed? And if so, was it still lying there? Worse, had it been turned to ashes?

'I – don't know,' he admitted.

'*Now* who's a daft mump?' screamed Alice. 'You don't *deserve* to be oldest – *I'd* never've lost it!'

'I'll . . . go back down and look.'

He did not much like the idea, with the dead dragon still steaming below.

'No!' said Griselda. 'We haven't got time. We've got to be home for dinner.'

The others realised that she was right. It felt like dinner-time. However long they had spent over the rim of the world – and they had no idea how long – they had not for a single moment thought of food. They had forgotten the real world, with its parks and schools and their own house in Lime Street. Now they were hungry. Ravenous, in fact.

'Dinner-time!' said Tom, and he kicked up towards the hole in the sky.

The bag would have to wait.

SEVEN

Once the children had eaten a dinner of burgers and chips followed by chocolate mousse, they were disgusted with themselves.

'How *could* we?' wailed Alice. 'Oh, what if we never see it again? That great big orange pussy-cat. I loved it, I did!'

'Oh leave off, Alice,' said Tom, who felt exactly the same. 'It's not the end of the world.'

'It is then!'

'The end of *that* world, anyway,' Griselda said.

'We never really looked properly for the bag,' Tom said. 'We could go back and look. The more I think *about* it, the more I'm sure I left it in the cave.'

'But we can't go there without the cat! How would we see?'

Tom thought.

'A torch?' he suggested.

'I suppose,' said Griselda dubiously. She remembered the fierce voice, the spiteful laughter, the echoes. Somehow, with the cat leading, she had felt safe. And it was not just because of the light that fringed its fur and lit their way, but because it seemed to have a kind of special power.

'We're not scared of those echoes any more,' Alice said. 'We know what to do. Just shout back at them.'

'And louder,' said Tom. 'Come on, it's our only chance.'

He found his torch and tested the bulb and batteries.

'The park *again*?' asked Mrs Dogberry as they set off. 'Well, at least you're getting some fresh air.'

'And flying in it, for that matter,' said Tom under his breath. His sisters giggled and their mother gave them a look.

'You're a silly lot,' she told them. 'Can't think where I got you from.'

'Was it in a bag under a laurel bush?' asked Alice.

'So it was,' she said. 'I remember now. Ought to have left you there.'

'Or given us to old Raggabow,' said Alice.

'Or that,' she agreed. 'Back at five, now.'

Lime Street was hot and dusty in the sun.

'Let's try something,' Tom said. He switched on his torch and shone it down on the pavement. 'See?'

'I can't see anything,' Alice said.

'That's just the point,' he told her. 'It's not as bright as the sun. But the *cat's* light—'

'It's always there,' said Griselda. 'Even in daylight, it's somehow brighter.'

'And remember how it lit the whole room up at night.'

'Better switch it off,' said Griselda. 'Save the battery.'

'Whatever—?'

They looked up, startled. It was the Murdoch, eyes like gimlets.

'A torch? In broad daylight?'

'Oh. Er . . . just switched it on by mistake,' said Tom quickly.

'But why are you carrying a torch? You are not going somewhere dark?'

The three studied their feet.

'I hope,' she said, 'that you have got rid of those disgusting bones.'

'Mum chucked them in the dustbin,' Tom said.

'*Threw* them, Tom. So I should hope. You had better tell me what you are doing with that torch.'

'Exploring,' said Griselda. 'We're pretending to be explorers.' This was true enough, in a way.

'Pretending? At your age? It's no use pretending in this world, Griselda, as you will no doubt discover.'

The trio stood and pretended to take note of what she was saying.

'Find something *useful* to do,' she said. 'Something sensible.'

'Yes, Miss Murdoch,' they chorused, and she gave them a hard, suspicious stare, then strode on.

'Old bat,' said Tom. 'Gone to do something useful, I expect.'

'Or sensible.'

'Or both!' said Griselda. 'Was *she* ever a child, d'you think?'

'Not if she's a witch, which she is,' Tom said. 'But if she was, I bet she was a sneak and a dobber and the other kids hated her.'

'Bet she wore clean socks every day . . .'

'And got all her sums right . . .'

'And never ran in the corridor . . .'

'Wonder what her first name is?'

'Rapunzel!' said Alice.

'No, silly! That was the girl's name, not the witch's.'

'All right, clever clogs, so what was the witch's name?'

'I can't remember,' Griselda admitted. 'I don't think she had one. Witches often haven't. They're just plain witches.'

'So she's just plain Murdoch,' Tom said. 'Suits her. The Murdoch.'

'She'd have a blue fit if she knew where we were really going with the torch,' Griselda said.

'Or if she knew we'd been flying,' said Alice. 'She'd never even believe it.'

'I hardly can myself,' Griselda said.

'Oh, and p'raps we never will again if we don't find the bag!'

'Shut up, Alice,' Tom said. 'Always whingeing. Whinge, whinge, whinge.'

Half the kids they knew seemed to be in the park, kicking, sliding, screaming.

'They're not doing anything sensible and useful,' Tom said.

'They're not having an adventure, either,' Griselda said. 'We are. They're on swings *pretending* to fly. We're really doing it!'

'Into the bushes smartish,' Tom said. 'Now!'

All three stepped sideways and were in the shrubbery and could smell the now-familiar odours of earth and greenery.

'Too much to hope the bag'll be back under the laurel, I suppose,' Tom said.

It was. By now they knew the special laurel from all the others. The ground beneath it was bare.

'So it's the cave now,' Tom said. 'If we can find it, that is, without the cat.'

'I think we can, now,' Griselda said. 'Just keep walking and we'll be there. That's all that happened.'

She hoped with all her heart this was true.

'Come on then,' Tom said. 'Let's do it!'

So they turned their faces away from the park and the real world and began to walk. And eventually they found themselves, exactly as before, in the deep dark wood. It happened between one step and the next, with a sudden darkening as the trees closed over their heads.

'We did it!' Tom was exultant. 'Stage one accomplished. Now for the cave!'

He led the way, and supposed that what he was doing was what people called 'following your nose'. In the past he had found that if he squinted slightly cross-eyed and downward, he could see the tip of his nose – just. He did not do this now, he just marched straight ahead and pretended to himself that he was following the cat. As before, the wood grew denser and darker. Then, just as he was about to admit that he might have lost his way, there ahead was the mouth of the cave.

They stood looking at it, glad that they had found it, but fearful of what was to come.

'It was only a voice, remember,' Tom said.

'Sticks and stones may break your bones but words can harm you never,' said Griselda.

'I'm going to sing really loud again,' said Alice. Nonetheless, she caught at her sister's hand as they stepped forward. Tom switched on the torch and it carved a path ahead.

'Not as good as the cat,' he admitted. 'We'll have to stay close together. Mind you keep up with me.'

The caves were darker than ever without the cat. Its light had been a radiance that spread; now they had only a narrow beam to follow.

They were expecting the voice, but jumped all the same when it came. 'Look out: *danger*! Look out: *danger*!'

It was not exactly brave of Tom to do what he did next, because he did it without thinking. He stopped dead and started to rake the cave with the beam of his torch.

'*You* look out!' he shouted.

The echoes of his own voice ran about them, but this time there was no answer. Whoever – or whatever – was stalking them was lying low.

'We know you're there!' called Alice.

There, there, there . . .

'But we don't care!' shouted Griselda.

Care, care, care . . . Then silence.

They began to walk on, and half expected the voice to start up again, but all they heard was the low muttering echoes of their own footsteps. Not one of them dared to turn and look over its shoulder.

Then, ahead, they saw a light thrown up on the roof of the cave, and knew they were coming again to the rim of the world.

They hurried forward and Tom was first. He began to play the beam of his torch over the littered rocks.

'Must be here, must,' he muttered. Then he saw it, half behind a boulder – Alice's tote bag. 'There!'

He ran and snatched it up and plunged his hand in and pulled out the mysterious grey bag that housed the cat.

'Look out!' screamed Alice.

Tom whipped the bag behind his back and next moment found himself looking up into the face of Raggabow.

'Give it here,' he snarled, and put out a hand to grab it.

'Shan't.' Tom stood his ground.

'Mine!'

'It's not. In any case, it's empty!'

'Oh no!' cried Alice. They were alone in this fearful cave with Raggabow. 'Cat, where are you?'

She might even have hoped the golden cat would appear in answer.

'You give me that bag or you're for it!'

'I thought you were meant to be a rag-and-bone-man,' said Griselda boldly. 'The bones aren't in the bag, so why d'you want it?'

'Empty now, maybe,' Raggabow said. 'Been empty before. But sooner or later that cat's back in the bag!'

He moved towards Tom, who backed away, still with the bag held behind him.

'Just leave us alone!' said Alice. Then she had a sudden inspiration. 'Go and get your own bones! There's millions down there!'

She pointed to the hole. The light from it streamed up into the cave, oddly lighting faces from below, giving them strange hollows.

'Go on! See for yourself!'

Raggabow did not look. On the contrary, he

took a few steps back from the rim of the world, and a shadow of something that might have been fear passed over his face.

'You daren't!' Alice was triumphant.

'He can't fly!' exclaimed Griselda.

'*We* can,' Tom said. He looked straight into Raggabow's flickering eyes. 'You clear off, or we'll just jump through that hole and take the bag with us!'

'You do that and you'll never see your mother again!' snarled Raggabow.

They stared. They could hardly believe their ears.

'What . . . what do you mean?' faltered Alice at last.

Did he mean to murder them, all three? She remembered their mother's warnings about bushes in the park.

'Lost your precious cat, ain't you?'

'Not exactly lost,' Griselda said. 'It'll come back.'

'Ah, but what if it don't?'

'It will,' said Tom.

'That down there,' Raggabow gestured towards

112

the streaming light at the rim of the world, 'that ain't nothing, not without the cat! And what's more, the cat ain't nothing without you!'

'We don't know what you're talking about,' said Griselda.

'Live in the real world, don't you?' said Raggabow. 'Live in a house and eat your dinners and teas and go to school?'

'Of course,' said Tom. 'So what?'

'I'll tell you what! *My* world, that is! Mine, and in my power!'

'You don't look much like a king to me,' said Griselda scornfully.

'You'll see,' he spat. 'You'll see!'

'In fact that gorgeous pussy's more like a king than you!' said Alice. 'And you haven't got a beautiful golden light.'

'I give you one last chance,' said Raggabow. 'Are you handing over that bag or not?'

'*Not*,' said all three together.

'No chance!' added Tom.

'So now you'll see who's king and who isn't,' said Raggabow. 'Just you try getting out of here now!'

He whirled and began to walk away. He walked out of the light streaming up from below, and into the darkness. He had no torch or lantern, yet he did not grope his way or stumble, but went as if it were broad daylight. The echoes of his footsteps ran around the rocks.

'He must be able to see in the dark,' Alice whispered, and shivered.

Next minute he was swallowed completely by the shadows.

'What did he mean, "Just try getting out of here"?' asked Griselda fearfully.

'Don't know,' Tom said. 'But I think we ought to get after him. We've got the bag, that's the main thing.'

'But it's empty!' cried Alice. 'What about the cat?'

'Look, the cat'll come back when it's ready. It has before.'

'That's why we can't give the bag to Raggabow. We daren't.'

'I wonder why he wants it,' said Tom. He began to stuff it again inside the tote bag, as if that gave it extra protection.

'I think I know why,' said Griselda. 'Because, once those bones are back in there, he'll keep it tight shut for ever! The cat'll never get out again.'

'It must!' said Alice. 'Oh, if I'd got a gun I'd shoot that horrible Raggabow!'

'Come on Alice, you know you wouldn't,' said Tom. 'And come on anyway. Let's see what he meant when he said we should try getting out of here.'

He started to walk away from the rim of the world and the darkness came to meet him. He switched on the torch and his sisters, with a last despairing look at the hole in the sky, hurried after him.

EIGHT

'There! We're out!' Tom stepped from the cave and switched off the torch.

They had made the return journey without the cat to guide them, and were safely out. They had not even heard the threatening voice and its echoes. Now they had only the forest between them and the park and the real world. The real, safe world. Griselda looked about and wondered whether she was only imagining that the forest was denser and darker than ever before. She tilted back her head and could see barely a glimpse of sky through the crowding branches. And — as before — there was that deep, uncanny silence and absolute stillness. They were in a place where no birds sang. It was hard even to imagine that beyond somewhere lay the ordinary everyday park, with its swings and bandstand and yelling children.

'But it does,' she told herself.

Alice too was looking doubtfully about her at the dense undergrowth, trying to make out the path.

'Wouldn't it be lovely if the cat suddenly came again!' she said.

Tom secretly thought the same, and gave the bag a swift shake in the hope of hearing the chink of bones. He did not expect any luck. And he knew that the cat had not deserted them, it was the other way round. They had flown up out of the other world with never a thought for the cat. In their eagerness for dinner they — or rather he — had carelessly left the precious bag lying where he had dropped it on the floor of the cave. Even now they were running away, frightened by Raggabow's threats. Somewhere that golden cat was alone, and being hunted.

'But we did one thing right,' he said out loud. 'We hung on to the bag.'

'What? Oh yes,' agreed Griselda.

'Back to the laurel,' Tom said. 'The cat might come again once we're there.'

'I don't think so,' said Griselda, but followed him anyway, with Alice close behind.

Again Tom followed his nose. It had worked

before and it would work now. He kept on, and hoped that suddenly he would find himself taking that last step that would bring him out of the dim forest and into the tame shrubbery of the park. Most of the time he kept his eyes down to avoid brambles and nettles, but each time he raised them the wood ahead was deep and dense as ever. No one had timed the journey from the laurel to the cave. No one, for that matter, had ever given time a thought once they had left the park behind. Now Tom did begin to think of time, and wondered. But he kept on, because after all that was the only possible thing to do. After ages and ages, he stopped and faced the others.

'I know,' said Griselda. 'We should be there by now.'

'P'raps we're going the wrong way,' suggested Alice.

'We seem to have being going for ages,' Griselda agreed. 'P'raps we're going the long way round, instead of as the crow flies.'

'There aren't any crows,' Tom said.

There were no crows or pigeons or any other kind of bird. That was part of the eeriness of the place.

'So now what?' asked Griselda, and he tried not to think of what Raggabow had said when he had glared at them with his red-rimmed eyes.

'Just keep on, I suppose,' Tom said. 'Bound to get there in the end.'

He turned and went on, wishing he had with him the compass he had asked for for Christmas, though he had a feeling that they were in a place that had no north and south and that the tiny finger would only have flickered wildly, useless. On and on they went.

'My feet are beginning to hurt,' Alice said.

'Oh, trust you,' Tom said. 'Whingeing again. What do you want to do, sit down and wait for a wolf to get you?'

'There aren't such things as wolves, are there, Grizzles?'

'Course not,' she said. 'Not in England.'

But were they *in* England? Were they in any place that appeared on a map of the world?

Again they stopped. Tom turned to face the girls, and saw from the corner of his eye something that was not a tree or thicket. 'I don't believe it!'

The girls turned to follow his gaze. There,

ahead, was the cave. And in its entrance squatted the unmistakable figure of Raggabow. He hugged his knees, watching them.

'Back where we started from!'

Unwillingly, because there seemed no choice, they went towards him. He grinned and showed his yellow teeth; his watery eyes flickered.

'Back again?' he said. 'Well, well, well! All that way and here you are again! Couldn't you find your way out?'

'You know we couldn't,' Tom told him. 'What's the game?'

'Oh, it's not a game. Oh no. Trouble with children, that is – forever playing games. And now look where it's got you!'

He rocked back and forth, gleeful and triumphant. 'Want to have another go? Better luck next time?'

They stared wordlessly.

'Or are you going to give me that bag?'

'No, we're not!' Tom's hold on it tightened.

'Never!' said Griselda.

'The cat's ours!' said Alice fiercely.

'Oh, is it?' sneered Raggabow. 'So where is it

now? Eh? The cat knows the way, but the cat ain't here!'

'Come on,' Tom said, 'let's go.'

They turned and went back into the dark wood and Raggabow's voice came after them.

'I'll get it in the end! Just you wait!'

'You won't, you won't, you won't!' Alice muttered under her breath, and thought of the shining cat, wondering whether they would ever see it again.

They had not gone far before suddenly it was cold. They all felt it at once, an enormous breathtaking coldness, a wintry air that had them shivering and bewildered, shocked by the wicked iciness.

'W-w-what's happening?' Tom's teeth were chattering.

They heard the first sound since they had entered the forest, a thin, piercing note that was the wind in the high boughs, and with it came the snow. It came in a white and dizzy dance through the dark lacings of the trees. They stopped and stood and wrapped their arms about themselves and shivered.

'I'm f-f-freezing!'

'W-what shall we d-d-do?'

Then they heard another sound, a long howl. And then another, and another.

'Wolves!' gasped Tom.

Alice screamed.

The baying grew louder, and they stood transfixed with the snow falling and thatching their hair white. The first wolf appeared. It stood with teeth bared and red tongue lolling. Its thick grey coat was tipped with frost. Other dark shapes assembled silently, slipping between the trees like shadows.

'Don't take your eyes off them!' Tom ordered.

He himself was staring into the mean gold eyes of the leader. He had read somewhere that as long as you stood your ground and held the gaze of any wild beast, you were safe. Griselda and Alice forced themselves to look too, though they really wanted to run.

'Now – back off! We're not far from the cave!'

He himself took a step backward, still holding his gaze on that of the wolf. The others followed suit. As they went backward the wolves came forward with slow menace. Every now and then one of them threw back its head and howled. Slowly, very slowly, the three retreated, sometimes half stumbling over a root, sometimes finding themselves hard against a trunk, but never once taking their eyes away from those of their pursuers. They were playing What's the Time, Mister Wolf? in reverse, except that this was a game in deadly earnest. The snow went on falling.

Griselda began to feel that she was drowning in a wolf's gaze, as if her eyes were locked for ever. But she dared not move them. The world was reduced to a pair of golden eyes in a flood of whiteness. She could hear Alice's little strangled sobs, and her brother's mutter, 'Back you brutes, back you brutes, back!'

She was growing dizzy, and prayed that she would not stumble and fall, pushing away pictures of a wolf at her throat, his breath hot on her face. She knew that they had not come far from the cave, but they were stepping backwards, and for all they knew were going round in circles. If that were so, there could be only one end to this grim game. Then, astonishingly, she felt warmth at her back.

'We're there!' cried Tom.

They had reached the mouth of the cave, and a great red fire burned there. Beside it crouched

Raggabow. All three ran into the cave and past the fire, and heard the wolves' furious snarling. Alice whirled on Raggabow.

'It was you. It was you that did it!'

He grinned. 'Did what, my pretty?'

'You beast, you beast!'

But the words were hardly out of her mouth when she saw — they all saw — that beyond the leaping fire lay only the deep dark forest. The snow had melted away, the wolves had vanished.

'Whatever——?' Griselda gasped.

'I don't believe it!'

'But there was snow and wolves. There *were*. We nearly died! You did it!'

'*You* did it,' replied Raggabow. 'You meddle with fire and you get your fingers burned.'

'We know you did!' said Alice hotly.

'Not me,' said Raggabow. 'It's that cat makes things happen, not me. And now look what it's done to you. As long as you go mixing with that cat you're bound for trouble. So why don't you give me that bag and get off safe back home?'

He stretched out a hand but Tom backed off.

'Come on, now,' Raggabow wheedled. 'You were all right before the cat and you'll be all right after.'

'But you hate it!' cried Alice. 'And it'll come back to the bag, it always does!'

'Oh, I'll not hurt it,' he said. 'Just want it back where it belongs, in the bag. You set off back into the forest and who's to say what you'll meet next time!'

The three stood silent, looking into Raggabow's face across the fire and with their own secret, fearful imaginings.

'You give me that bag and you'll be out that forest safe as houses before you know it.'

Tom hesitated. He was beginning to wonder if Raggabow was speaking the truth. As he had led the way in the forest he had thought how awful it would be if they became lost. He had begun to wonder whether, although it seemed so silent and lifeless, dangers lurked there. Wild beasts . . . wolves . . . Had *he* conjured up the wolves, by imagining them? And was that because he was carrying the mysterious bag?

'Do you promise?' he heard himself say.

'I promise!' said Raggabow eagerly.

'And the cat – you've got to promise not to hurt the cat!'

'I promise!'

Still Tom hesitated. He turned to Griselda. 'Shall I?'

'After all, the cat's not *in* it,' she said slowly.

'And he has promised. Cross your heart and hope to die?' said Alice.

'Cross my heart and hope to die!' agreed Raggabow.

Griselda thought again of the forest blotted out in snow, the baying of the wolves, and their cruel fangs.

'Go on then,' she said.

Silently Tom held out the bag. In an instant, Raggabow snatched it and started to dance, now hugging it, now shaking it. His shadow danced madly with him in the firelight.

'Got it, got it! Oh my beauty, *now* I've got you! Dead, dead, dead!'

They watched, horrified. He danced and stamped and twirled, and seemed to have forgotten they were there at all.

'Now what've we done?' Griselda felt cold and sick.

'But he *promised*!' said Tom.

At last Raggabow twisted to a standstill. He grinned at them and his eyes were red as the fire.

'Got you!' he hissed. 'Got the cat and got you! Get off now where you belong, all of you.'

They stood motionless.

'Go on. Get off!' He stamped his foot.

'What about the cat?' said Griselda.

'Like to know, wouldn't you? I'll see to the cat. You get off home.'

'You promised,' cried Alice.

'Hah! Poof! What's a promise?'

'Crossed your heart and hoped to die.'

'Poof! Course I did! Worked, din't it?'

They were appalled. Promises could not be broken. They were sacred. There was something powerful in a promise, something binding. And now this awful creature had made and broken one within the minute, and was actually glorying in it.

'Come on,' said Tom grimly. 'Back into the cave.'

'What? *What*?'

'To find the cat,' Tom told him. 'You've tricked us, but you haven't won yet!'

'You get off home! You hear me? The cat's dead!'

'I don't believe it,' said Griselda. 'I think it's still there over the rim of the world, and we're going to find it!'

'Rescue it!' added Alice.

'Ah,' sneered Raggabow, 'all very fine. But you ain't got the bag and you ain't got the cat. You go over the edge of the world and – he flung out his arms – 'down you go! *Bang*!'

'We can fly!'

'Could,' he said. '*Could* fly.'

'Come on!' said Tom. He walked away from the fire and switched on the torch.

There was no bodiless voice on this journey. At first they heard Raggabow screaming after them, 'Look out, look out! You'll never get back!'

They marched on, though their hearts were beating hard. Through the rocky cave they went for the second time that day, following the narrow beam of the torch. At last they saw the streaming light ahead and knew that they were there again at the rim of the world. When they reached it they dropped wordlessly to their knees and gazed down through the hole in the sky, far above the dried-out valley. They were looking hungrily for a bright splash of gold. They saw only what they had seen that first time – bones and rocks, rocks and bones.

'Puss!' called Alice. 'Come on – puss, puss!'

The word drifted forlornly and hissed in the crannies of the cave.

'So now what?' said Griselda.

'We fly!' said Tom.

'Oh, Tom – dare we?'

'Don't you remember what the cat said, that first time? It said if we wanted to go into the other world we had to be brave.'

'Very brave,' added Alice. 'And I'm not sure if I am.'

They stared silently down at the strange other world. Each was thinking the same thought. This time, if they stepped off the edge into that sky, they might drop like stones.

'The cat will help us,' Griselda said.

'But Raggabow said it was dead!'

'I don't believe him,' said Griselda. 'How can you believe anyone who breaks promises?'

'If we leave here now,' said Tom slowly, 'if we go back, I don't think we'll ever see the cat again.'

The thought was unbearable. The cat had come into their lives and shaken their whole world like a kaleidoscope. The pieces had flown into a wild new pattern.

'I'll go first,' Tom said. He was the oldest, and again wished that he weren't.

'No!' said Griselda. 'We'll jump together. Hold hands!'

NINE

They joined hands, Alice in the middle, and it was a kind of comfort. A long, long way below lay the valley of bones. Griselda swallowed hard.

'I – I think we should all wish as we jump. Wish to fly.'

As a rule, she kept very quiet about wishes.

'All right,' agreed Tom surprisingly. 'Can't do any harm, I suppose.'

'I never get what I wish when I blow my candles out!' said Alice unhelpfully.

'That's different,' Griselda told her. 'This is for real. Ready? I'll count to three, then jump!'

'Wait!' said Tom. 'What about Mum?'

They thought about their mother and their house in Lime Street, and it all seemed light years away.

'I mean, if we don't come back!'

'Don't say that!' squealed Alice. 'I was just getting brave and now you've made me frightened again. And I think I'm getting wobbles in my tummy!'

'We've all got them,' Tom told her. 'Only some of us don't make such a big deal of it. I just think we ought to leave a note or something.'

'Daft mump!' said Alice. 'And leave it where?'

'Here, I suppose.'

'Oh *yes*!' said Griselda. 'She's *always* coming here! It's the first place she'd look!'

'All right, sarky,' said Tom. 'I still think we should. Think what she'll be like if we don't come back.'

'You're doing it again!' Alice tugged her hands free and stepped back from the edge.

'I'm going to do it anyway.'

He produced a Biro and dug in his pockets for an old shopping list. The others watched in dumb misery as he wrote. It occurred to both of them that it was still not too late to turn back. After all, as Raggabow had said, they had been all right before the cat, and could be all right again. The trouble was that they could never be the same again, not really.

Tom finished writing, then looked about for a small stone to anchor the note.

'What have you put?' Griselda asked.

'You know. Sorry and all that.'

'And love!' said Alice. 'Did you put lots of love from us all?'

'Course!'

He stood up again and put out his hands, and his sisters each took one. Again they stood at the jagged edge of the hole in the sky.

'Same as before,' Griselda said. 'Ready? One – two – three!'

On 'three', they all jumped, their eyes shut tight. As the ground went from under their feet, they felt the air embrace them – and hold them!

'We did it!'

'We're flying!'

'Woweee!'

They opened their eyes and dropped hands. Tom let out a yell and began a kind of victory dance in the air, and the others too soared and spiralled and swam effortlessly as fish in water. They wove their separate patterns in the air and, just as before, wanted to stay there for ever, because it was so easy and impossible that it was like living in a dream.

It was Griselda who remembered first why they

were there. She began to dive down, all the while keeping her eyes fixed below in the hope of a glimpse of gold. Down and down she went and the valley of bones came up to meet her. Now she could see their separate shapes – rib, skull, backbone, leg – and then—

'Quick!' she screamed. 'The cat!'

Tom plunged past her in a steep dive and Alice came paddling furiously, arms spread.

'There!' Griselda pointed to a patch of ginger, abrupt against the grey.

Next minute they felt the ground under their feet and stood breathless, staring. The cat lay motionless by a great rock.

'Asleep,' said Alice. 'Let's wake it!'

They picked their way carefully towards it. Griselda was thinking that it looked strangely small, and seemed to have lost its shining.

'Cat!' she called. 'It's us! We're coming!'

It did not even lift its head, and she felt a little clutch of panic. 'It's dead,' Raggabow had said. 'Dead, dead, dead!'

The eeriness of its stillness struck them all with a chill. The cat was a creature of movement, with its proud walk and waving tail. Now it was slumped, eyes closed, and the light that always surrounded it was barely visible. In fact they were not sure that it was there at all. They went slowly now, on tiptoe, breath held.

'Cat,' said Griselda softly. 'Cat, wake up! It's us!'

But the eyes were squeezed tight shut, there was not so much as a twitch of an ear to show that it had heard. They gazed down at it dully, and dared not say what they were thinking.

At last Alice dropped to her knees beside it, she peered into the familiar whiskery face and tears were rolling down her own face, though she did not bother to brush them away.

'Oh cat,' she whispered. 'Dear cat, what have we done?'

She put out a hand and plunged it into the deep softness of its fur, and two other hands came out and did the same. They stroked it, all three, and Tom was muttering, ''S my fault? 'S my rotten fault!'

'It's all our faults! We should never've done it, oh we should never've done it!'

'We're sorry, we're sorry!'

Alice was sobbing now in earnest, though she never for a moment stopped stroking. Nor did any of them, as if they secretly hoped they could stroke it back to life. They knelt among the bones and smoothed the warm fur that they might never see or touch again, and no one said anything. There was utter silence throughout the dry valley.

And then, miraculously, there was a faint sound, and at the same time a vibration: they felt it through their fingertips. They raised their heads and stared at one another in disbelief and then, as the sound grew louder and the vibrations stronger, joy.

The cat was purring! They kept stroking and smiled, beamed broadly at one another, so hugely relieved that they could not help it. The purr was not the deep lion roar they had heard before, but it did not matter. The cat was alive.

'Puss!' said Alice softly. 'Wake up, it's us!'

The cat's eyes opened, ever so slightly, two shiny yellowy slits. But it did not stretch and yawn and rise to its feet.

'You came back,' it said, so weakly that they barely caught the words.

'Course we did!' said Tom gruffly.

'We couldn't go without you!'

'We did what you said,' said Alice. 'We were really brave and we jumped and then we could fly again!'

'I was nearly done for,' whispered the cat. 'If you hadn't come back—'

'It was that horrible Raggabow, it was his fault!' said Alice.

'No,' murmured the cat. 'Not all his fault. What have you done with the bag?'

They exchanged looks over its head. None of them wished to be the one to confess. When they looked down, the cat had closed its eyes again.

'We've done something awful—' began Griselda.

'We had to!' said Alice. 'We couldn't get out of the forest and there were these ravening wolves, and—'

'And he *promised*!' said Tom. 'He promised not to hurt you!'

'You gave him the bag,' said the cat, eyes still closed. 'I knew it. I knew it in my bones.'

'But we could get another,' said Griselda eagerly. 'We could get you a nice new one, and . . .'

Her voice trailed away. The cat was looking at her and slowly shaking its head.

'It won't do. I must have it back or . . . *die.*'

They were horror-struck.

'That is where I must go to renew my power. I must keep going to the bones before I can come to life again. Hadn't you guessed?'

They shook their heads dumbly.

'So what shall we do?' cried Alice despairingly. 'Raggabow's got the bag now. How shall we ever get it back?'

'And he's gone back to the real world,' said Griselda. 'He says that the real world belongs to him. Does it?'

'Oh yes,' said the cat. 'And if I die, all this world, too. That is what he wants, has always wanted. He has hunted me . . . hunted me since the world began . . .'

Its voice grew fainter, its eyes closed again.

'Don't die, oh please don't die,' begged Alice. Her eyes were beginning to spill again. 'We'll do anything, just tell us what to do!'

'There is only you . . . who can keep me alive now. You must not let me go . . .'

'We won't!'

'We swear!'

'You cannot stay here. You must take me back with you, back to your world. I am . . .' Its voice grew fainter still. 'I am tired now . . .'

They stared down at it, and could hardly believe how it had changed from that shining creature that had first appeared from the bones. They remembered how the skeleton had performed a slow dance in the air, and how the cat had taken shape in a light that had filled the room. Now it seemed curiously shrunken and dull.

'We'll have to carry it.' Tom knew it, *and* that he was the one to do it. He held back because the creature was so magical that he was timid at the thought of lifting it, holding it.

'Go on, then,' said Griselda.

Uncertainly he reached and lifted, and the cat was strangely light, so light that even Alice could have picked it up. He cradled it in his arms and felt its soft warmth.

'Back up now,' said Griselda.

'You'd better not drop it!' added Alice.

'You'll have to help me,' Tom told them. 'My arms aren't free.'

The others each took one of his arms.

'On "three",' said Griselda. 'One, two, three!'

They all pushed upwards, Griselda and Alice pointed their free arms and they were airborne. They rose slowly, and this time there were no aerobatics, just a long straight upwards dive towards the hole in the sky. No one spoke. They stared down at the slumbering cat and beyond that the receding valley, its bones melting into a blur.

When they came again to the rim of the world, Tom said, 'You take the torch, Grizzles. Better not wake the cat.'

Griselda felt in his pocket and found the torch.

'The note!' said Alice. 'The note for Mum! Thank goodness we didn't need it!'

She took the paper from under the stone and stuffed it into Tom's pocket.

Griselda led the way. The beam carved a path in the darkness, and every now and then she flicked it left and right, half fearing that Raggabow was still somewhere about. At last she saw the mouth of the cave ahead. There was no sign of Raggabow, or the fire that had been burning.

'Look!'

Alice's tote bag lay there. She ran and picked it up and peered in, and saw straight away that the cat's bag, the one that mattered, had gone.

'At least you won't have to explain to Mum why it's gone missing,' Tom told her.

'Shall we . . . Shall we put the cat in this one? It might get used to it and like it.'

'No,' said Griselda. 'You heard what it said. Come on quick, let's get back to the laurel.'

The forest they must travel through had lately harboured wolves. Twice they'd tried to get out of it and failed. No one knew what tricks Raggabow might have up his sleeve.

But they had the cat with them, and this journey through the wood was safe. It was not long before they found themselves making the one particular pace that took them back into the park and the real world. Utter silence gave way to the muffled sound of traffic and children's voices.

They stood uncertainly by the laurel.

'Now what?' asked Griselda. 'This is where

the cat belongs, but we daren't leave it here, not now.'

'No fear!' said Tom. 'But if we take it home, what's Mum going to say?'

'And what if it gives her asthma?'

That was the reason the Dogberrys could not keep pets.

'We can tell her it's a stray,' Griselda said. 'True, anyway.'

'And put it in the shed,' said Alice eagerly. 'She wouldn't mind that – not for a bit, anyway.'

Tom stared down at the cat in his arms. 'Funny the way it seems smaller now. And lucky, I suppose, it's not shining. Mum's not blind. She'd see it wasn't an ordinary cat.'

'But it looks fairly ordinary now,' Griselda agreed. 'So that's what we'll do. Mum's bound to feel sorry for it. She likes cats, even if they do give her asthma.'

They slid out from the bushes and on to the path and headed for home.

'Oh stink!' said Alice.

'I don't *believe* it!' added Tom.

There, again, was the Murdoch. It was as if

they were attracting her like iron filings to a magnet.

'Just say hello and keep walking,' said Griselda, as she started to force her own face into a smile.

But the Murdoch was looking at them, and at Tom in particular, and frowning. 'Tom!'

They stopped. They had no choice.

'Yes, Miss Murdoch?'

'Tom Dogberry, whyever are you walking in that peculiar fashion?'

'I . . . What do you mean?'

'With your arms held in that ridiculous way!'

She was looking at Tom's arms, that were cradling the cat, and *she did not see the cat*!

'I, er, I've got a sort of cramp.'

'Rubbish!' she snapped. 'Hold them properly!'

Tom hesitated. He could not bring himself to drop his arms and let the poor sick cat fall to the pavement.

'Do you hear me?'

Tom was desperate, but in a flash Griselda snatched the cat from his arms and at once he dropped them to his side.

'Whatever—?'

The Murdoch was flummoxed by this extraordinary manoeuvre, but her attention was distracted by the piece of paper that fluttered from Tom's pocket. Alice saw it too, and stooped to pick it up, but was not fast enough.

'It's private!' she cried, but the Murdoch was already reading.

'"Dear Mum, this is a note from all of us to say we're sorry . . ."'

'It's *rude* to read other people's letters!'

'". . . We've gone over the edge of the world, but we had to, to save the cat. We think you'd have wanted us to if you knew the story. We all hope you'll forgive us, and lots of love from Tom, Griselda and Alice."'

The Murdoch looked up.

'Whatever nonsense is all this? What do you mean, 'gone over the edge of the world'? Is this some kind of silly game?'

'Yes,' said Griselda quickly. 'Just a game we were playing.'

The Murdoch eyed her narrowly.

'Griselda,' she said, 'now *you* are holding your arms in that peculiar way!'

This time it was Alice's turn to snatch the cat, and this time she started walking, because sooner or later the Murdoch would be bound to put two and two together, even though four, in this case, was an impossible answer.

TEN

At last Tom and Griselda were free of the Murdoch, though not until after she had delivered a stern lecture on their general silliness.

'I sometimes wonder if you live in the real world,' she told them, and stalked off.

'Horrible old bat,' said Tom. 'She's still got my note. What if she goes to Mum again?'

'We'll say the same,' Griselda told him. 'Just a game we were playing. But . . . oh Tom – *she didn't see the cat!*'

'I know. Spooky or what?'

They started to walk to where Alice was waiting. She had obviously been thinking about this, too.

'Listen!' she said. 'If she didn't see the cat, Mum won't either! We can take it up to one of our rooms. It'd hate being left alone in the shed.'

'Where Raggabow might find it,' Griselda added.

'But even if it is invisible it still might give Mum asthma,' Tom objected.

'It didn't before,' said Alice. 'It was under your bed for ages.'

'But it was in the bag most of the time,' Tom pointed out. 'You don't get asthma from bones.'

'Well, I think we should,' Griselda said. 'It's ordinary cats Mum's allergic to. You can't call this one ordinary.'

They gazed at the cat, still slack and sleeping in Alice's arms, and tried to remember how huge and bright it had once seemed.

'I want to have it in my wardrobe,' Alice said. 'I'm going to make it a little nest. You'd like that, wouldn't you, puss?' She dabbed under its chin.

In the end it was agreed.

'But if Mum starts wheezing, we put it in the shed,' Tom said. 'Take it in turns to guard.'

'What – even at night?' Griselda pictured the darkened garden, the sleeping houses, and Raggabow on the prowl. She shivered.

'Come on,' she said. 'Let's do it. You run straight upstairs, Alice.'

As it happened, Mrs Dogberry was in the garden, weeding. Alice ran upstairs while the other two poked their heads round the back door.

'Hi, Mum!'

'We're back!'

'Blessed dandelions!' she said. 'You wonder where they come from. Have a nice time?'

'Great,' said Tom, and grinned at Griselda.

They had encountered wolves and flown in the sky of another world, and their mother asked if they had had a nice time!

They went up and found the cat lying on Alice's bed like an improbable nightdress case. She was already on her knees by the wardrobe.

'I'm using T-shirts, mostly,' she said. 'They're softest.'

'It's been asleep an awfully long time,' said Griselda. She peered closely and was reassured to see the rise and fall of its breathing.

Alice reached past and gently lifted the cat.

'There!' She gazed at the cat in its nest. 'Isn't it sweet? I've always wanted a pet.'

'Yuk!' said Tom.

'It's not a pet!' added Griselda sharply.

'It wasn't before, but it is now,' Alice said. 'We're looking after it. That makes it a pet.'

'It does not,' said Griselda. 'It's a brilliant, amazing beast, so don't you go treating it like a hamster!'

'And it's not safe just because it's in your wardrobe,' Tom told her. 'You heard what it said. We've got to get that bag back.'

'But how?'

'We don't even know where Raggabow is.'

'And we can't go looking because it's nearly teatime.'

'And after that it's starting to get dark.'

'I just wish it would wake up,' said Griselda.

But the cat did not wake up, and when they came up again after tea it was still sleeping. They went down and watched television, and tried not to think of Raggabow out there somewhere in the darkness, still hunting the cat.

By the time they went to bed they were becoming fearful. The cat had not opened its eyes once since they had left the other world.

'But we did right to bring it with us,' Tom said. 'In fact, it told us to.'

Alice had fetched a saucer of milk and set it by

the wardrobe door, but it did not seem to have been touched.

'You'd better hide that, Ally,' her brother said. 'It'll take some explaining if Mum sees it.'

'In any case I don't think the cat would drink it,' Griselda said. 'I don't think it eats or drinks at all.'

'I know what you mean,' Tom agreed.

Usually the cat had such energy that it gave off light, but it was hard to believe that its source was sardines or kippers, and saucers of cream.

'Things die without water,' Alice said. 'Without milk, rather.'

'Usually, yes,' said Griselda. 'D'you think . . . D'you think it would help if we stroked it again? Talked to it?'

'Yes, let's!' said Alice. 'I'll lift it on to the bed so's we can all get round it.'

'Let me!' said Griselda jealously. She had held the cat in her arms only for a few moments and it was, after all, she who had found the bag of bones in the first place.

She lifted it gently and was surprised by its lightness. It was as soft and warm as she had imagined. She held it for a moment, then placed it on Alice's bed, and it sank into the duvet.

'I think we should turn the light off,' Tom said. 'Then, if Mum comes in, she won't see us.'

'Oh what a wise Thomas!' said Griselda. She clicked off the bedside light.

The room went into darkness, and on the bed there was the gleaming blur that was the cat. It was faint, hardly more than a shimmer, but it came from within and wasn't the effect of the streetlight on its coat.

'It's still got a shining,' whispered Alice. 'Come on, let's make it purr again.'

Their hands went out gingerly. Because of the shining they were rather shy, as if they were doing something without first asking permission and were being overfamiliar. Steadily their three hands flattened the dense fur. They went in a slow rhythm and hardly ever did their hands touch, as if they had rehearsed. As they did so their thoughts were not very clear, but were mainly silent messages to the cat, or strong wishes.

Griselda wished so hard that she instinctively shut

her eyes tight, but her hands kept moving blindly over the warm fur.

'Look!' Alice breathed.

Griselda opened her eyes and saw that now the cat was giving off a soft radiance, and in it she could plainly see the intent faces of the others, lit palest gold. Wordlessly they carried on, disbelieving of their own success. The cat was not purring as it had before, but this was even better, this steady strengthening of the light. No one dared speak, for fear of breaking the spell. In the silence they could hear footsteps on the pavement below, muffled voices from the television downstairs.

The cat moved. It stretched and yawned and then all at once it lifted its head, and with a graceful spring was on the floor, leaving the stroking hands in midair.

'Hurray!' cried Alice.

The cat went stalking about the room as it had that first time, inspecting it, treading carefully between dropped trainers and jeans.

'So, here I am again in the real world,' it said at last, and turned to face them.

Alice remembered that this was exactly what had

happened before — and then the cat had walked out of the window and into the night sky.

'Oh, you're not going, are you?' she pleaded.

'I have nowhere to go,' the cat replied. 'Thanks to you. And I shan't last long here.'

'Whyever not?' asked Griselda, alarmed.

'You can't stay up all night stroking me, I suppose,' it said.

'*I* could,' said Alice. 'I wouldn't mind a bit.'

'You'll go to bed and fall asleep and dream.'

They looked at it, not knowing what they should say. If it asked them to stay awake all night, they were quite prepared to try.

'Do you like the nest I made for you?' asked Alice, avoiding the question. She indicated the crumpled T-shirts at the bottom of the wardrobe. The cat eyed them disdainfully.

'Raggabow will never find you there,' she went on. 'You could stop there for ever. You could—'

'No!' The cat drew itself up and its light glowed more intensely. 'I am a visitor here just as you are in my world. Did you enjoy your visit?'

They had almost forgotten the events of the morning. Had they really raised a sheep and a fire-breathing dragon from the bones, and watched St George battling from a bird's-eye view in the sky?

'I'd forgotten that,' admitted Griselda. 'But thank you.'

'Me, too,' said Tom. 'That was an ace dragon.'

'You didn't think so at the time,' Griselda reminded him. 'Who tried to fly up to escape?'

'It was me that made St George!' said Alice. Then, to the cat, 'But where did you go?'

The cat shrugged.

'What you do when you get there is your own affair,' it said. 'Nothing at all to do with me. I merely led you there. And now, of course, you can get there by yourselves.'

'It was brave of us, wasn't it?' said Alice. 'We honestly didn't know if we could fly or not.'

'We were scared stiff,' Tom admitted.

'And even left a note for Mum in case we didn't get back.'

'Which the Murdoch's got,' added Tom.

The cat seemed to be hardly listening to any of this. It had sprung on to the windowsill and was staring out, up at the sky above the roofs and chimneys.

'Shall I ever get back?' it said mournfully, and with the words the halo of light around it seemed to dim a little.

They stood uncertainly in the darkening room and felt a kind of fear, as if Raggabow were actually near, perhaps even coming up the stairs.

A soft tread *was* coming up the stairs. For an instant they froze, then, 'Quick!' gasped Griselda.

She hadn't time to feel awestruck this time. She snatched up the cat — whose shining must surely be visible — plonked it on its nest and slammed the wardrobe door. She streaked to her bed, jumped in and had just pulled up the duvet when the door opened softly.

'Asleep?' asked Mrs Dogberry softly.

It was Tom who answered. She was, after all, bound to discover that he was not in his own room. 'No, actually. Just talking.'

'In the dark?'

'Telling ghost stories,' said Griselda quickly, and crossed her fingers to cancel out the fib.

'What a funny lot. Don't you go frightening Alice.'

'I'm not frightened!' said Alice. 'Not of silly old

ghosts, anyhow,' she added, then she too crossed her fingers.

'Come along now, Tom.'

'OK.

He went without fuss. The girls lay and listened for the sounds that meant their mother was getting ready for bed. At last the crack of light below their door disappeared.

'Come on!' Griselda was out of bed, but Alice was there first and opening the wardrobe door. Their clothes hung there weirdly lit from below – jeans, dresses and jackets as familiar as their own skins – yet suddenly awkward and scarecrow. Below crouched the cat, and its eyes were wide and yellow.

'Don't be scared,' said Alice. 'Only Mum. She wouldn't hurt you even if she did see you.'

'She's a pussy-cat,' said Griselda. 'Oops – sorry!'

'You could come out now and sleep on my bed, if you like,' said Alice.

'No!' said Griselda. 'But we'll leave the door half open.'

The cat gazed up at them without speaking.

'You will . . . You will still be here in the morning?'

'I told you. Without you, I should die now.'

They hated it saying that.

'Well, you've *got* us,' said Alice.

'Now you will go to sleep and dream,' it said. 'You are safe from Raggabow in your dreams.'

'Unless they're nightmares,' said Alice. 'I get nightmares sometimes.'

'Dreams are the enemies of Raggabow,' the cat said. 'Remember that. And remember you are the only ones who can save me now.'

It seemed to be trying to tell them something.

'The trouble is,' said Griselda, 'you can't choose your dreams. They choose you.'

'Perhaps,' said the cat. 'Perhaps . . .'

It yawned and they saw the pink of its throat.

'I am tired now . . .' It closed its eyes.

They gazed for a little while, then each lightly touched the dense fur and softly said, 'Goodnight,' then turned and went back to their beds like sleepwalkers.

Griselda lay wide-eyed and saw the room by the muddy sodium of the streetlights and that one soft beam from the half-open door of the wardrobe. She thought about what the cat had said about dreams.

'If I could choose a dream,' she thought, 'it would be one that showed me where Raggabow is, and how to get the bag back.'

She tried to solve the problem herself. She guessed at places where Raggabow might be hiding, but she could not even begin to imagine where. All she could picture was Raggabow himself, with his red-flecked eyes flickering in the firelight. She saw herself combing the streets of the town, but whenever she thought that he might be hiding behind that door or that tree, the pictures misted over, and all she saw was the grinning Raggabow, flaunting the precious bag.

She felt that now she dared not go to sleep for fear of nightmares. With a huge effort she tried to picture the cat as it had been when they first saw it. It worked. At first she saw only snatches, but at last the figure of Raggabow faded, and instead she saw the jigsaw of bones performing their slow dance in the air. Then the cat came, as huge and amazingly gold as ever, and perhaps that was the moment when she finally drifted into sleep.

She thought afterwards that it must have been, because now she found herself following the cat through the streets of the town. It threaded between the walking people and she knew that it was invisible to them, and perhaps she was, too. They went past the Butter Cross and Town Hall, past Woolworths and the Oxfam shop. She saw them from the corner of her eye, but her gaze was fixed on the plumy tail of the cat.

It turned off the main street and into a row of little brick houses, with brightly painted doors and window boxes. Griselda followed. She did not know why, but knew that she must follow the cat to the ends of the earth, or till the cows came home.

The cat stopped by one particular house. It was neat and trim with a shiny, grey front door and net curtains. The cat sat and waited. It gazed at the door, and Griselda knew that she was meant to knock. She stepped forward and lifted the black knocker, *rat-tat-tat*.

The door opened, and there stood the Murdoch. Griselda stared aghast but could not speak, and realised that the old enemy could see neither herself nor the cat, but was looking up and down the street with the frown that thousands of children had seen and dreaded. Then, surprisingly, she banged her front door shut and started to walk up the street.

Now there were three of them going Indian-style: the Murdoch, then the cat, then Griselda. The busy world was going on about them, but only like a silent film. On they went, and then they were in Lime Street and going past her own house, and that was when she realised that they were going to the park. Single file they passed through the high wrought-iron gates. There were children everywhere, soundlessly screaming and running and kicking. The Murdoch did not look left or right, but kept on along the path that led beside the shrubbery. She reached the place where the children had left the path to find the laurel. She stopped. The cat stopped and so did Griselda.

The Murdoch turned her head and gazed across to where the bandstand stood near by. There was Raggabow. He squatted on the steps and rocked to and fro, hugging the stolen bag. He looked up, straight at the Murdoch, and grinned. Then he waved the bag triumphantly and the Murdoch went towards him.

This time the cat did not follow. It stood with

its back arched, fur on end. Griselda tried to lift a foot, but it would not move. She was frozen there. All at once the world went into slow motion. The Murdoch was moving towards Raggabow and he towards her, and Griselda watched helplessly as she saw . . .

Griselda lay for a minute, and knew that she was in her bed and that it was morning.

'Oh no!'

She had been within a fingertip — a whisker it seemed — of solving the mystery. It had all been so real that she wondered if she had been really walking the streets of the town in her sleep.

'Grizzles! Grizzles!'

She opened her eyes. Alice was sitting bolt upright in bed, her eyes wide.

'This dream! I had this amazing dream!'

'Me too! I was following the cat and—'

The door opened and Tom rushed in. 'Hey, I wait till you hear this! I had this dream and—'

'Is it still there?' Griselda scrambled up and went to the wardrobe. There on its crumpled nest lay the cat. It looked large and plump as if it had grown in the night, feeding on dreams. It glowed in the dimness of the wardrobe.

'Thank goodness! But listen—'

'No, *you* listen—'

It was a long time before anyone listened to what anyone else was saying. But when everything was unscrambled it turned out that they were all trying to say the same thing. They had all had an amazing dream.

'And I knocked on the Murdoch's door!'

'No, *I* did!'

'It was me! I did! It was grey and shiny and—'

'And she came out, but she couldn't see me or the cat!'

'And then we followed her—'

'No, *I* did – you weren't there!'

'And nor were you!'

They were all furious at the hijacking of their private dreams. But slowly they came to realise the impossible truth.

'Hang on,' said Tom. 'So where was Raggabow?'

'In the bandstand!' Griselda and Alice spoke in chorus.

They looked at one another, all three, still fuddled by sleep and their minds hardly working.

'I don't believe it!' said Tom at last.

'We all had exactly the same dream!'

'We *can't* have!'

But they had. They had all followed the cat through the town, all knocked at the Murdoch's door, all gone in silent procession to the park, and all – maddeningly – woken up at exactly the same moment.

'It's spooky!' said Tom.

'We could be in *The Guinness Book of Records*!' said Alice.

'Except you can't prove dreams,' Griselda told her. 'No one would believe us.'

'What I don't get', said Tom, 'is why we weren't in each other's dreams. I mean, we're all in this together, so why weren't we all there?'

They pondered.

'People don't take much notice of other people's dreams,' said Griselda. 'I mean, if just I had had that dream and told it to you two—'

'We'd just have thought it was a silly old dream,' said Alice.

'Right,' said Tom. 'You do have some daft dreams, Grizzles.'

'So we all had to have the dream for ourselves,' said Griselda. 'And I suppose you can't be having a dream and be in someone else's dream at the same time, especially if it's the same dream.'

This sounded like double-Dutch, even to herself. They pondered again. It was all very confusing. None of them knew very much about the laws of dreaming, or even whether there were any rules at all. The one, simple inescapable fact was that they had all had exactly the same dream. Griselda looked over to the wardrobe.

'Wonder if the cat had the same dream?' she said.

'And the Murdoch . . .'

'And Raggabow . . .'

They looked fearfully at one another. They did not like the idea of entering the dreams of their enemies. What was worse, they did not know how their shared dream had ended.

Eleven

The cat still had not woken when they went down to breakfast. They longed to wake it and tell it about the night's adventures, but did not like to. For all they knew, it was having important dreams of its own.

'I've had Miss Murdoch on the phone,' their mother told them. 'What exactly are you up to?'

'What did she say?' Tom countered.

'You should know perfectly well. It was you who wrote the silly thing. What's all this about the edge of the world, and not coming back?'

'A game!' said Alice and Griselda together.

'She's worried about you, and so am I. First that bag of bones and then — and what's all this about a torch? I thought you were all in the park.'

'We were.'

'Playing this game.'

'It sounds a funny kind of game to me. If

you ask me, you'd better keep away from the park if—'

'No!'

'Oh no!'

She looked at them long and hard.

'Some game you've thought up I suppose, Griselda.'

'Not exactly.'

'Well, whatever, you'll have to give it a miss. We're going into town this morning.'

All three bit hard on their tongues. To protest would give too much away.

'You all need new shoes. And what was that about your school skirt being tight, Griselda?'

'It's mine!' said Alice. 'Mine's too tight.'

'You can have Griselda's, and I'll get her a new one.'

'I hate being the youngest,' said Alice. 'Horrible old cast-offs!'

'There's years of wear in that skirt yet,' said Mrs Dogberry. 'And I can take it in if it's too big.'

'I'm just a walking scarecrow,' Alice said. She glared at her sister, who always got the new clothes, though Griselda had pointed out long ago that it was hardly her fault. She had even said that she wouldn't mind swapping places. 'Then you'd have my silly name, and I'd have yours!' Griselda would say.

On that occasion Alice had secretly thought that perhaps she had got the better of things. After all, clothes are always being changed, but a name is for life.

'We'll go at about nine,' their mother told them. 'Give you a chance to tidy your rooms first.'

The young Dogberrys exchanged looks. This would give them time to consult the cat and plot their plots.

'And I want you dressed properly. Do you hear me?'

When they went back up, the cat was sitting on its nest in the wardrobe and gazing in a sad, bewildered way around the room.

'Oh puss, you're still alive!' said Alice rather tactlessly.

'Of course,' replied the cat, 'and shall live for ever, if I'm properly treated. I have been here since the beginning of the world, remember.'

'Of course,' said Griselda, 'and we have tried to treat you properly.'

'You gave the bag to Raggabow,' said the cat sternly.

'Only because he promised——' began Tom, but the cat interrupted him.

'On the other hand, I do believe you meant me no harm. That was an excellent dream we had.'

'We? You mean you——?'

'Of course,' replied the cat. 'I was there, wasn't I? In fact, it was my dream. I simply shared it with you.'

They did not argue. They had, all three, privately thought of the dream as their own, and were secretly miffed that the other two should have had it, too. But they were happy for the cat to claim it.

'We know where Raggabow is now,' said Tom.

'And that he's in with the Murdoch,' added Griselda.

'But we can't go to the park!' wailed Alice. 'We've got to go shopping.'

'Shopping?' said the cat. 'What is that?'

It was hardly likely to know, living as it did in

a place of dry bones that could flash into life at the dab of a paw.

'You won't leave me? Don't leave me!' Its face was suddenly pinched.

'We've *got* to,' said Griselda desperately.

'You mustn't! I told you, I shall die without you!'

They stared, miserable and helpless.

'P'raps one of us could pretend to be ill and stop behind,' suggested Griselda.

'Daft mump! We've all just had our breakfast, haven't we?' said Tom.

'And in any case, Mum would never leave us alone, not if we were ill,' Alice said.

The cat lay down and curled on its crumpled heap of T-shirts as if already resigned to its fate.

'Think of me,' it said. 'Even if you are not here, think of me. Hold me fast.'

'Oh we will, we will!' promised Griselda, who was beginning to understand that what went on inside your head was just as important as what went on in the real world. She turned to the others. 'All do it!' she ordered. 'Wherever we go and whatever we do, think of the cat!'

'Think of me shining,' murmured the cat, whose eyes were already beginning to close.

'Oh, dear, beautiful, shiny cat, of course we will!' Alice promised.

They heard Mrs Dogberry coming upstairs and swiftly pushed the wardrobe door closed. They knew that she could not see the cat, but couldn't quite believe it. Invisibility was a very hard thing to grasp.

'Your new jeans, please,' she told Tom. 'And Alice, get your hair brushed.'

Alice gazed at her, wondering whether now would be a good time to have a wobbly tummy. On the whole, she thought not. She had been told that she went very white on such occasions, and did not think that she was up to acting white.

Half-heartedly the three got themselves ready. When their mother reappeared, she was looking unusually smart.

'Come along!' she said briskly. 'We've got a—' she broke off and smiled unexpectedly. 'Let's go!'

Griselda was last out, and before she went she pulled open the wardrobe door. The cat's eyes were closed.

'Shan't be long,' she whispered. 'And we'll think of you!'

It's not going to be difficult, she thought. Shopping for clothes, especially school clothes, was not the most riveting experience in the world. She followed the others down and was already silently saying, 'Cat cat beautiful cat, cat cat shining cat,' and thought she could easily keep this up all morning, or even for ever, if the cat's life depended on it.

They set off along Lime Street, past the gates of the park. As one, their eyes swivelled sideways. They could just see the curved sides of the bandstand through the trees. Then it had gone and they were heading for the town.

'You're all very quiet,' their mother remarked.

She was not to know that they were all fiercely picturing their beloved cat, trying to see it in all its golden shining.

So deep were they all in their private imaginings that they hardly noticed where they were, and followed their mother up the High Street and past the windows full of shoes and trainers, past the clothes shops and W. H. Smith. Tom was seeing the slow dance of bones in his room that first night, Griselda the cat glowing like a lantern in the dark cave, and Alice the moment when the cat had launched itself into the night sky and walked on air above the dark roofs of Lime Street.

It was Griselda who first noticed that there was something odd about this shopping trip. 'But we've gone past all the shops!'

They were approaching the railway station.

'Where are we going?'

Mrs Dogberry stopped. She smiled widely. 'Guess!'

'You said we were going into town.'

'Ah, but I didn't say *which* town!'

'But—'

'Surprise, surprise!' She was delighted with her success in fooling them. 'London. We're going to London!'

Her children, jolted out of their daydreaming, stared blankly back at her. This was not at all what she had expected. She had pictured their delight and excitement, their eagerness to be on the train and off on their adventure.

'Ah – Mrs Dogberry!' The voice was unmistakable. 'How odd to meet you when we've just been talking!'

'Yes, isn't it?' said Mrs Dogberry weakly. She herself was not particularly keen on the Murdoch, who seemed to think that children should be kept cleaner and neater than was humanly possible.

'Looking very neat and tidy.' The Murdoch surveyed the trio and they gazed blankly back. 'Going somewhere special, are you?'

'To London,' their mother told her.

'Ah. Off for the whole day, then.'

They would be far away in London all day, while the Murdoch and Raggabow would be there – and the cat defenceless in its hiding place.

'That will be educational for them,' went on the Murdoch, and she was almost smiling. 'May I suggest the Science Museum, Mrs Dogberry? Or perhaps the National Gallery?'

'I . . . We'll see,' said their mother. 'We must dash, I'm afraid, or we'll miss our train.'

'Oh, we don't want that,' said the Murdoch.

'*She* doesn't want that, she means,' Griselda

whispered to Tom as they went into the station. 'Just our luck! We're always running into her.'

'Or her into us,' said Tom grimly. 'Now she knows the coast's clear.'

'But she can't get into our house!' Alice was shocked.

'Raggabow could,' said Tom. 'He could get in round the back. I wouldn't put anything past him.'

'What shall we *do*?'

Their mother was already buying the tickets. There was nothing they could do.

'That's the worst of being children,' said Griselda bitterly. 'You always have to do what the grown-ups want. Even for treats.'

'Listen,' said Tom, 'the main thing is to do what the cat asked us. Think of it. Think of it every single minute!'

The others nodded. It was all they could do. They set off for London full of this resolution.

At first they managed quite well. They were always excited to be on a train, and usually this would be part of the treat. They played all kinds of games, such as seeing who could be first to count ten churches in the sliding landscape, or guessing whether the next church would have a tower or a steeple. Now they sat quietly in their seats and hardly glanced out of the window. Alice actually had her eyes shut. Their mother was mystified. She was not to know that Alice was flying in the sky of another world with a miraculous golden cat.

'Are you feeling all right?' Perhaps they were sickening for something.

The three nodded.

'Fine, thanks,' said Tom, seeing not his mother but a flat, whiskery face with yellowy slits for eyes.

'Now – any ideas where to go?'

Mrs Dogberry waited for the expected rush of suggestions; the squabbles, even. Nothing. 'Well, we did the Tower last time, and in any case there'll be terrible queues with it being half-term. I suppose there will be everywhere.'

She began to feel that it was very hard work giving these particular children a treat.

'Of course, if you haven't any ideas we can always go shopping for school things. There'll be more choice in London.'

This suggestion worked.

'Oh no!' said Alice, who was not in line for anything new anyway.

'You're joking!' said Tom.

'Madame Tussaud's!' said Griselda quickly.

From that moment on they were more or less lost. They were, after all, only human. It is a hard thing to do to keep a picture in your mind when you are looking forward half fearfully to the Chamber of Horrors, or when your mother dips into her bag and brings out a book of teasers and puzzles. Then, when they reached London, there was the exciting ride on the Tube, rattling and swaying through the darkened tunnels. Once or twice they remembered the cat, but its image had soon gone. In any case, it now began to seem so far away and impossible, it might have been a dream after all.

Once inside the waxworks they were lost, mesmerised by the uncanny gaze of the still figures, so lifelike it was only their stillness that gave them away.

'I think if someone famous stood there and didn't move, everyone would think they *were* a waxwork,'

Alice said. 'In fact, for all we know, someone could be at this very minute.'

It was not impossible. Griselda herself felt slightly uncomfortable staring at the figures, having been brought up to believe that it was rude to stare. She was particularly careful not to stare too hard at royalty.

Only when they reached the Chamber of Horrors did they briefly remember the cat. It was dimly lit in there, and perhaps the darkness reminded Tom of the cave, because he whispered, 'Raggabow ought to be in here!'

Even as he spoke, he guiltily remembered their promise to the cat. The others did too, and they tried to force a memory. A glimpse of it floated into their minds and then was gone.

By the time the train was halfway home it was growing dusk. Trees and hedges were shadowy shapes and lights twinkled from the houses. Alice fell asleep. Griselda nudged Tom.

'The cat!' she whispered, and he nodded.

She closed her own eyes and thought properly

of the cat for the first time since they had left that morning, and felt a pang.

'We forgot it,' she thought. 'How could we?'

She tried to make up for lost time, though she knew that was impossible, that long hours of the day had passed with the cat out of sight and out of mind.

'Let it be safe,' she prayed. 'Let it be safe!'

The house in Lime Street was in darkness when they arrived back there, sleepy now and chilly.

'A quick drink and straight to bed, I think,' said Mrs Dogberry, as she opened the door and switched on the light. 'It's been a long day.'

They blinked in the sudden brightness at the familiar kitchen, with the red check cloth covering the table, and knew with a jolt that they were back home and the day behind them was already only a memory. All that mattered now was the cat.

'I'm going straight to bed,' said Tom, and the others said, 'And me.'

'Had a nice day, did you?'

They assured her that they had, but their look was so strange and anxious that she thought for the hundredth time what a queer lot they were. It was almost as if they lived in another world.

The wardrobe door was half open as she had left it. Even so, Griselda was fearful, because there was not even the faintest gleam of light shafting from it. Slowly she advanced and peered round the door.

The cat was still there, but she knew at once that something was wrong. It lay curiously shrunken and limp, and the once-bright coat was dull.

She knelt, the others behind her.

'Cat,' she whispered. 'Cat!'

There was no response. The cat lay still as any waxwork.

'Oh puss,' said Alice. 'What's wrong with it? Wake up, puss!'

'It won't,' said Tom. 'It's too far gone.'

Griselda felt an unbearable welling misery. 'I didn't think of it!' she confessed. 'Hardly at all.'

'Nor me.'

'Me neither.'

They were no better than Raggabow. They had made a promise and broken it. They stared down in silence at the still form.

'We could . . . try stroking it,' Alice said at last.

Tom shook his head. 'Too late for that.'

Griselda knew he was right. She knew that she could not bring herself to lift the moveless form because what she was thinking, and trying not to think, was that the cat was dead.

TWELVE

Griselda did not even see the cat in her dreams that night. And yet, when she awoke, it was her first thought. Her eyes went straight to the wardrobe door, still half open. She did not jump up and run to it as she had yesterday. Then the cat had been plump and shining. She did not think she could bear to see the small, faded creature lying there in the full light of day. Tears squeezed from her eyes. The cat had come into their lives of its own free will and offered them a whole new world. All it had asked was for them to keep it safe, and they had failed it.

We're murderers, she thought. *We're as much murderers as the ones in the Chamber of Horrors.*

She lay for a while crying softly. They could not leave the cat where it was for ever. They would have to bury it. And there was only one place possible: beneath the laurel where she had first found the bag of bones.

Raggabow won, in the end, she thought. *I hate him. I'd like to kill him.*

She had already killed the thing she loved. She saw again the cat's flat, whiskery face and its yellow eyes, and sobbed afresh. The sound must have woken Alice.

'Grizzles?'

Griselda could not answer, and next minute Alice was there, clinging and crying too. 'I can't bear it, I can't bear it!'

'It was the best thing that ever happened in our whole lives.'

In the end they got up and went slowly to the wardrobe, dreading what they would see. There lay the crumpled heap of clothes. *The cat had gone.*

They could not take it in. Had the cat, already small and shrunken, shrivelled away to nothingness in the night, leaving not a trace that it had ever existed? It seemed impossible, but so was it for Raggabow to somehow enter the house and come creeping in the darkness to snatch his prey. In any case, the cat was already dead.

Griselda ran across the landing into Tom's room.

'Quick!' she hissed. 'Come quick!'

He sat up, and she saw that his eyes were pink.

'Come on!'

He scrambled up and followed her. Silently she indicated the empty wardrobe, where Alice still stood stunned and staring.

'Gone!' he said blankly. 'It's impossible!'

'Everything about it was impossible,' Griselda said.

'Raggabow!' said Tom. 'I could kill him, *kill* him! Come on, get dressed!'

'But—'

'We've got to *do* something!'

'But what?'

'I don't know — anything! Hurry!'

They pulled on their clothes and went downstairs; softly, so as not to wake their mother. Tom quietly turned the key of the back door and they were out in the early morning freshness. There was only one place to go.

The street was deserted. There was little danger that they would run into the Murdoch this time. They ran as if every second counted, but did not know why – except that even now they could not quite give up hope.

'Stop a minute!' Tom gasped as they reached the iron gates. 'Listen. We've still got to get that bag back! And remember what the cat said? Raggabow can't get to the other world.'

'Yes, but—'

'But the cat could come here, into the real world!'

'In a way,' said Griselda. 'No one else could see it.'

'It doesn't matter. Those bones in the other world, we made them come alive. We made them into anything we wanted!'

Still they did not see what he was saying.

'What if . . . what if we made them come alive, and *they* could come here!'

'What? The sheep you mean, and—'

'No, idiot! Something – I don't know – dangerous! Something to make Raggabow give back that bag!'

'But – we don't know we can still *get* to the other world,' Griselda said. 'Not without the cat.'

'There's only one way to find out. We've got to,

we've *got* to! What if the cat went back to bones in the night, and now it's *in* the bag, at this very minute!'

Griselda gasped. She had not thought of that. Nor had Alice. 'And we could still save it!'

'Yes!'

They would try it. It was their only hope.

'Quiet, now,' Tom warned as they entered the park. 'We'll check the bandstand first. See if he really is there.'

It was strange to be in a deserted park. In the distance was a single man jogging and they could hear a dog barking. The swings dangled empty. They went cautiously over the grass towards the bandstand, leaving footprints in the dew.

He was there. He lay with his head on a folded sack, his dirty fingers clutching the precious bag even in sleep. Griselda nudged Tom and raised her eyebrows. Could they not simply snatch the bag, here and now? He frowned and shook his head, then turned and made back to the path.

'Too risky,' he said in a low voice when they were out of earshot. 'And we'd only have one shot. If he woke—'

Griselda knew that he was right. Here, in the real world, Raggabow was king. They could only guess what powers he might have. Into the bushes they went and towards the laurel where it had all begun.

'Just keep walking,' Tom said, when they reached it. 'It's still there, all of it. Must be.'

So they kept walking, each of them willing the forest still to be there, and then they made the one step that took them from the tidy shrubbery of the park into the dense undergrowth and darkness that meant they were in another place.

'We did it!' Tom was exultant. 'I told you!'

They began the now-familiar journey through the forest in the dim greenish light. The only sounds were the crack of twigs, the brush of leaves and their own breathing.

It was only when they reached the cave that they realised that they had no torch.

'Oh no!' wailed Alice.

'That's torn it!' said Tom. 'Have to go back, I suppose, and by then Raggabow could have woken up. Oh *blast*!'

Griselda took one or two paces into the cave.

'We can't go in without it!' came Tom's voice behind her.

Cautiously she took a few more paces, then stood. As she stood, she realised that the darkness was not as dense as she had thought. It had only seemed so by contrast with the light outside.

'I think we can,' she said.

'No. I daren't!' cried Alice.

Griselda went back and took her hand.

'You try,' she told Tom. 'Go in a little way and let your eyes get used to the dark.'

He went in.

'See what you mean,' he said. 'But we're still near the entrance, remember.'

'It'll just get darker and darker!' Alice said.

'Think of the cat!' Griselda told her sternly. 'And remember what it said. About being brave.'

'We can try,' Tom said. 'If we have to turn back, well, that's it. I'll dash back home and get the torch and—'

'But Mum could be up by now!' Griselda reminded him. 'And she'd want to know where we were and . . . oh, it'd never work!'

'So it's go or nothing,' said Tom slowly.

'Yes.'

'Look, Alice, I'll go ahead. You and Grizzles keep close behind.'

'Go on, then,' Griselda told him. 'Let's try it.'

So they entered the cave, and in the beginning it was just as Griselda had said. They could see, however dimly, as if by a kind of prickly starlight. But with each step they took, that faint light drained away, and at last they found themselves in utter darkness. Tom stopped.

'This is it,' came his voice. 'Can't see a thing.'

Thing, thing, thing . . . ran around them.

The darkness was horrible, it was like a living thing, powerful and threatening. Walking in it was like stepping into a tiger's cage or towards the edge of an abyss.

'We're stuck halfway. There's light behind us and we know there's light ahead, but we don't know how far ahead.'

'I feel as if I've disappeared,' said Alice in a small voice. 'And you.'

'Listen,' came Tom's disembodied voice. 'We'll keep going on. Just shuffle your feet forward. Don't take actual steps. Just shuffle.'

They heard the scuffing of his own feet. Centimetre by centimetre he shuffled forward, or rather what he hoped was forward. They could go round and round in circles like explorers in the snow. They were in a huge nowhere, a no-man's-land.

Tom's toe encountered something hard. He put out his hands and groped as if he were playing Blindman's Buff. They met a cold, hard surface.

'Wait!' he ordered. 'We're up against a wall or rock or something.'

He remembered once reading that if people are blindfolded and start walking, they will almost always veer to their left. They can hardly ever walk in a straight line, and nine times out of ten they veer left.

'Listen, go to the right!'

'I've forgotten which *is* right!'

'Just keep hold of me.'

Tom turned away from the invisible barrier and shuffled to his right. He tried to picture a straight path ahead, the narrow beam of a torch. Then he shuffled ever so slightly to the right of that path. He realised that Alice was right. In total darkness you know which is your left foot and which

189

your right, but the idea of leftness and rightness disappears.

He inched his way onward. The only sound was the scuffing of shoes on stone and the little muttering echoes. Again his foot encountered something hard. Again he put out his hands. 'Oh no! We must've hit the other side!'

'Oh, how much further? I don't think we'll ever get out now. I think we'll be here for ever and ever and—'

'Shut up, Alice!' Tom told her. 'We're going forward, that's the main thing, even if we are zigzagging. When you move this time, move left, but not too far left.'

'Listen,' said Alice, 'I've just thought of something really terrible.'

'You would! What?'

'We can't go back now even if we want to, because we don't know where back is. And you keep saying "go forward", but you don't know which way is forward any more than I do!'

Tom knew that she was right. He couldn't be sure they were moving forward, however gradually.

'It's like being in outer space,' said Griselda. 'Or – or a black hole.'

'Just shut up saying things like that!' Alice's voice sounded trembly, as if she was fighting back tears.

'No. Sorry. Didn't mean it.' Griselda squeezed her hand. 'It was what you said about feeling as if you've disappeared. I feel like that as well.'

'And me,' came Tom's voice.

'But we *haven't*! If any of us were here on our own, then we might really believe it, but we're not. I know you're there and you know I am, so we can't have disappeared!'

Her last word hissed about them like an invisible snake.

'Raggabow came through here without a light,' came Tom's voice. 'He must be able to see in the dark.'

Dark, dark, dark . . .

The echoes died and in the silence they thought about this awful truth.

'And – how do we know the hole in the sky is still there?' quavered Alice. 'Now that the cat's gone, perhaps that's gone as well.'

'I don't believe it!' said Griselda. 'The cat said

191

once we'd been shown it we could go there any time we wanted.'

'Did it?' said Tom. 'I don't remember. It's so dark I can't even *think*!'

'We can't just stand here,' Griselda said. 'We must keep moving.'

'I've just thought of something really terrible.' Alice sounded as if she were going white. 'What if . . . What if the hole in the sky is still there, but . . . but when the cat's light went out, *that* light went out as well, in the other world.'

'Trust you to think of that,' Tom said, but he felt a rush of terror. They did not know what rules governed that strange other world. Certainly not those of the real world, where human beings could not fly, but where you could count on the sun rising and setting.

'Let's get on.' He started to shuffle again, this time with the fear that the next move might take him over the edge of the world, where he would plunge in darkness down to the valley of bones.

Slowly, fearfully, they inched their way forward. They did not speak, each for the same reason. Their eyes were open but sightless, so all three tried to see the cat in all its shining, as it had been when they first saw it.

When they came near the rim of the world, they saw it this time from a long way off, because of the absolute darkness. They saw the light shafting up like the sun behind inky rain-clouds.

'We're there!'

Now they could see, and they hurried on. When they reached the shattered roof of the sky, they dropped to their knees and saw the other world. They stared down, hungry for a glimpse of gold that would mean all was not lost, that the cat had somehow found its own way back there.

'Not there!' said Alice.

'Now what?' Because of the darkness and terror of their journey through the cave, Tom had half forgotten what his plan had been.

'What you said!' Griselda told him. 'Go down and bring some bones alive! Make them into something terrible, then see if we can get them back.'

'Not wolves,' said Alice. '*We'd* be scared, not just Raggabow.'

'Yes,' admitted Griselda, remembering.

'But we've still got to get back through the

cave,' Tom said. 'And we still won't have a light.'

'Think of something, quick!' pleaded Alice. 'For all we know, Raggabow's woken up and he might even have gone.'

'*You* think of something,' Tom told her. 'The only thing I can think of is glow-worms, and a fat lot of good they'd be!'

'Oh wow!' said Griselda softly. 'Wow! I think I've got it!'

They looked at her.

'We need a light to get back, and we need to scare Raggabow. I think he was frightened of the cat!'

'That's why he wants it back to bones and in the bag!'

'So what if we . . . I know *our* cat's not there, but what if we—?'

'After all, I raised a dragon!'

'Yes.'

'Let's do it!'

They did not hesitate. All together they launched themselves into the sky and were flying; and because they were there and flying, they knew that Raggabow had not won yet.

'We'll all do it!' Tom shouted. 'We won't just raise one.'

'Dozens.'

'*Hundreds.*'

'Thousands.'

Down they floated, light and free as never before after that terrifying darkness. They all touched down together and hesitated for an instant, looking at one another.

'Do it!' commanded Tom. 'Come on – let's do it!'

He bent down and touched a bone, and Griselda and Alice did the same. This time there was no slow dance of bones. Three cats sprang up in the instant, as bright and gold and hugely furry as ever their own had been. They stretched and yawned and gazed about them.

'Hurray!'

'Again,' yelled Tom. 'Again!'

They darted here and there among the bones, and at each touch of a finger another cat sprang up. They did not stop to look or count, they were dizzy with their own power, they felt like lords of creation.

'There. There. There!' Griselda made three cats with a single sweep of her arm.

'Another, another, another!' Alice was chanting.

Cats were springing up about them like mushrooms, jump started by the touch of a fingertip.

'Stop,' gasped Tom at last. 'Stop!'

He straightened up.

'Wow! Oh wow!'

All about them the valley had gingered over. An army of cats stood licking a paw or preening a whisker. There was a softly waving sea of fur.

As the three stood awed by what they had done, one by one the cats grew still. They stood quite motionless and gazed back with their yellow eyes.

'They don't know what to do,' Griselda whispered. 'Tell them!'

Tom drew a deep breath.

'Listen,' he began. 'We want you to help us.'

'Please,' added Griselda.

'It's this Raggabow, you see,' stammered Tom, unnerved by the battery of eyes. But the eyes were mild, so his courage grew and he told them of the plan to rescue the precious bag. They seemed to be listening, ears pricked.

'It's our last chance,' he ended. 'Will you help us? *Please*!'

A purring began, a great purring chorus from a hundred and more cats, each larger than life and each with its own halo of light.

'You *will*!' screamed Alice.

'Let's go,' yelled Tom. 'Quick as you can!'

He pointed up his fingers, palms together and pushed off, and the others followed suit. The cats took to the air and swam with paddling paws and plumy tails curved up. They flew in a dense impossible flock, among the children, and above and below them.

When they reached the hole in the sky they streamed through it, and Tom saw that the cave was already filled with light.

'This way.' He wove his way through and the girls followed. 'Left right, left right!'

He marched forward and the cats swarmed with him.

'It's all lit up like Christmas!' Alice could hardly believe that only minutes ago the cave had held such terrors. Now the walls and roof were softly lit and harmless.

'I can't believe this is happening!' It seemed to Griselda that after this anything could happen. They were on their way back to the real world with an army of shining cats, and for all they knew those cats would be visible for the whole world to see. What a commotion there would be when they hit the park, what screams and stretching of eyes!

It'll blow everything! she thought. *They'll find out about the other world*. She did not care. She cared only about that shabby grey cloth bag she had found under the laurel bush.

Then they were out of the cave and into the forest, and that was lighter than it had ever been – almost sunlit. The cats plunged through bracken and brambles, swift and purposeful. They could not speak like the cat from the bag, but must have understood what Tom had told them because they moved like cats going to a rescue. They kept together and their light went in a broad sweep with them.

The cats crossed the invisible line into the real world and still they kept going. Tom had to run to keep up.

'We're nearly there,' he shouted. 'I'll show you!'

Griselda and Alice were hemmed in by cats, unable to run.

'It's happening,' Alice kept saying. 'It's happening!'

Tom burst out of the shrubbery on to the path and pointed at the bandstand.

'There! He's there!'

The cats came streaming out in a long wave and Tom thought there should be trumpets, a great triumphant burst of music. Even now, in broad daylight, their coats were fringed with light. Already a handful of children were on the swings or kicking balls, and not one of them so much as turned or pointed. The everyday world was going on exactly as usual. No one so much as blinked an eye at the explosion of cats. Not, by now, that the Dogberrys cared.

Tom raced over the grass and Griselda screamed after him, 'Grab it. The minute he wakes up, grab it!'

But there was no chance. The cats were streaking now like tigers, stretched to twice their length, and were already reaching the bandstand. Then came a high terrified scream. There was Raggabow, struggling to his feet and looking frantically about him. He held the bag clutched to his chest.

The cats swarmed about him, blocking his escape.

'Look – his eyes are shut!'

Those eyes that could see in the dark could not bear the light of the multitude of cats.

Griselda pushed her way forward. It was she who had found the bag and it was she who should get it back.

'Give me that bag!' she commanded.

Raggabow, his eyes squeezed tight, wrapped his arms around himself and cowered, but still held on to the bag.

'Or else,' said Tom. He turned to the cats. 'You can do it! Make him!'

The cats began to hiss. They arched their backs and hissed, and those at the front prowled forward.

'You're trapped!' screamed Alice. 'You'll never get away.'

As she spoke, a cat sprang. It jumped right up, paws against Raggabow's folded arms, and he let out an agonised scream and the bag dropped. Griselda snatched it up.

'Hurray!' yelled Tom and Alice. Then '*What*—?'

Griselda straightened in time to see the impossible.

Raggabow was collapsing. The features of his face melted like running wax. His head lolled sideways and his arms dangled. In slow motion he crumbled, down and down until at last there was only a jumble of rags and bones. The hissing of the cats became a chorus of purrs.

Griselda, Tom and Alice stared at the grubby heap as that, too, dwindled and faded and at last vanished. Raggabow had disappeared into thin air.

Tom turned to face the cats who stood in a great swirl of gold against the green. 'You did it!'

Griselda, still stunned, looked down at the bag she was holding, and shook it gently. There was a soft chink and slither.

'It's there,' she whispered. 'The cat's back in the bag!'

'Griselda Dogberry! Tom!'

The voice was unmistakable. The Murdoch was up and about early. The three of them looked at her, and then at the mildly gazing army of cats, and could hardly take it in. There was a miracle happening under her very nose and *she could not see it*. If she could behave as if the cats weren't there, they could behave as if she weren't, either.

'Whatever's going on?' she said. 'What's all this yelling and shouting?'

There was no point in explaining. They had just beaten Raggabow and could beat her.

'Better go back now,' said Tom to the cats. 'You've done it – and thanks!'

'Thanks. Oh thanks!' cried Griselda, and Alice leaned forward and touched the bag with her fingertips.

'Oh, it's true. It's back!'

The cats turned, they wheeled in a great orange arc and the Dogberrys watched because such a sight had never been seen in the park before and probably never would be again.

'I think you had better give that dirty thing to me,' they heard the Murdoch say.

'Sorry,' Tom said, without moving his eyes from the retreating cats. 'We need it, see.'

'For this game we're playing,' added Alice, and her eyes were fastened on the cats, too. They were the only things that mattered. The Murdoch was an alien, from another world.

The cats streamed on. The leaders had reached the shrubbery now.

'Did you hear me? Did you *hear* me?'

They watched hungrily, wanting the moment to last for ever. They watched so that they would never forget that a tribe of orange cats had once invaded the park, had shattered its ordinariness and made it magic.

'Tom! Griselda!'

Now the last of the cats were weaving between the clipped bushes and back towards the wilderness of the forest and, beyond that, the rim of the world. Their coats flashed and glistened as the sun came out. They longed to follow, to go straight to the laurel and tip out the bones and see again that flat, whiskery face with its yellow eyes. They dared not – not yet. Raggabow had gone, but there was still another enemy.

Tom looked at the frowning Murdoch, then grinned at his sisters. 'Come on! Three times round the park, then you know where!'

He started to run and the others followed.

'Tom, Griselda! Come back this minute! You hear me?'

They heard her but they did not care. Their beautiful golden cat was back in the bag and soon, very soon, they would see it again. They had almost lost it once and didn't mean to again.

They kept running and their feet thudded over the dewy grass so that light flashed from their heels. They ran till the Murdoch's voice had faded, but did not stop till they had reached the far side of the park. They turned, panting, and looked back.

'There she is!'

They saw the back of her, making for the park gates.

'Gone to tell Mum, I bet!'

'Wish we'd let the cats get *her*!'

'Would *she* have melted to nothing?'

None of them knew.

'We can go straight back to the laurel now she's gone!'

And so they did, walking now, because of the poor cat's bones. Griselda cradled the bag and whispered, 'Nearly home!'

'Weren't those cats amazing?'

'Raggabow's face!'

As they approached the path by the shrubbery they fell silent. Their hearts hammered. In silence they crossed the path and went into the shrubbery and pushed their way through the springing boughs towards the laurel.

They reached it, and it looked like any other laurel in the world. Griselda dropped to her knees and looked inquiringly up at the others. Tom nodded. Gently she tipped the bag and the bones came slithering out and lay in a jumble.

'Please, cat, we'd like to see you.' Her voice was wobbly.

'Please, please!' breathed Alice, and squeezed her eyes shut as if in prayer.

She opened them in time to see the magic, though. They all saw the slow dance of the bones as they reared and turned and floated in air. And they all saw the skeleton made flesh – or rather fur – until the cat was there in all its prodigious furriness and glowing with its own private light. They gazed at the flat, bewhiskered face and into the golden eyes. They were filled with such joy and lightness that it seemed that they might actually take off and fly. They had woken that morning to a world gone horribly dark and cold, a world without the cat. And now it was back.

'Oh cat!' whispered Griselda.

Alice said nothing, but bent and scrabbled her fingers in the dense coat as tears dripped off her nose.

'We're sorry,' said Tom in a gruff voice. 'About leaving you, and that.'

The cat seemed to be smiling, and Alice's fingers had woken its purr.

'Raggabow's gone,' said Griselda. 'Gone for ever!'

The cat nodded its great golden head. Then it turned and began to stalk away, making for home.

Tom made to go after it but Griselda caught his sleeve.

'Leave it,' she said. 'Plenty of time later.'

And so there was — all the time in the world. Griselda picked up the bag, folded it neatly and pushed it out of sight under the laurel.

'We've got all the rest of our lives now,' she

said. They knew their own way to the edge of the world, and Raggabow was dead.

The Dogberrys too turned and went, with their faces turned to the real world — and breakfast.